SINCE YOU ASKED . . .

SINCE YOU ASKED...

maurene goo

SCHOLASTIC PRESS • New York

Published by Scholastic Press, an imprint of Scholastic Inc., *Publishers since 1920.* SCHOLASTIC, SCHOLASTIC PRESS, and associated logos are trademarks and/or registered trademarks of Scholastic Inc.

Library of Congress Cataloging-in-Publication Data

Goo, Maurene.
Since you asked / Maurene Goo. — 1st ed.
p. cm.
Summary: Fifteen-year-old Holly Kim, the copyeditor for her San Diego high school's newspaper, accidentally submits a piece ripping everyone to shreds and suddenly finds herself the center of unwanted attention — but when the teacher in charge of the paper asks her to write a regular column her troubles really start.
ISBN 978-0-545-44821-5
1. Korean American teenagers — Juvenile fiction. 2. Student newspapers and periodicals — Juvenile fiction. 3. Journalism, School — Juvenile fiction. 4. High schools — Juvenile fiction. 5. Popularity — Juvenile fiction. 6. San Diego (Calif.) — Juvenile fiction. [1. Korean Americans — Fiction. 2. Newspapers — Fiction. 3. Journalism — Fiction. 4. High schools — Fiction. 5. Schools — Fiction. 6. Popularity — Fiction. 7. San Diego (Calif.) — Fiction.] I. Title.
PZ7.G596Sin 2013
813.6 — dc23
2012034891

10 9 8 7 6 5 4 3 2 1   13 14 15 16 17
Printed in the U.S.A.   23
First edition, July 2013

The text was set in Caecilia.

To Katherine Emma Hong

ONE

. . . .

BHS BACK IN SESSION,
INEVITABLE HUMILIATIONS TO ENSUE

Holly, don't you think you should at least wear a new pair of jeans for the first day of school? Why don't you dress up anymore?"

I rolled my eyes and took a deep breath. She was starting already. "Mom, I'm not in first grade. No one dresses up for the first day of school anymore. Don't listen to those JCPenney commercials."

As the words came out of my mouth, my eleven-year-old sister, Ann, walked into the kitchen looking like a "Back-To-School Cool!" advertisement in a JCPenney catalog. Her long hair was pulled back with a hot-pink headband that matched her hot-pink tank top, and she wore a long gray cardigan and black leggings. On her feet were black Chucks complete with hot-pink laces.

My mother looked pointedly at her and then at me. I glanced down at my gray hoodie, perfectly distressed skinny jeans, and flip-flops. I shrugged. "Ann's still optimistic about life." Mom rolled her eyes and went to finish getting ready in the bathroom.

Ann walked over to the refrigerator, where she pulled out a gallon of milk. And like every other morning before school, I pulled out two huge glasses. She poured milk to the very top of each glass, and then we chugged it all down.

I let out a loud dairy-induced burp. Ann countered it with an even louder burp. We laughed devilishly.

"GIRLS!" Mom hollered from the bathroom.

"WHAT? You're the one who makes us drink this every morning! Don't you know that Asians are naturally lactose intolerant?" I hollered back.

Mom rushed in, dressed in a suit, pulling curlers out from her hair and grabbing her purse. "I'm SO sorry that I work ten-hour days and don't have time to make you spoiled brats a fancy breakfast like all the other moms do!"

I shook my head. "Wow, guilt projection much?"

She grabbed her keys and gave me a no-nonsense glare. "I don't know what you're talking about, but be quiet and hurry up because we're ALL going to be late!"

Ann and I grabbed our backpacks and ran out the front door, jumping into the car as it was practically rolling down the driveway already. If anything, our mother was always efficient.

"Okay, Ann, do you know where to go for your first class?" Mom asked as she put on her makeup and eyed the traffic signal at the same time.

"Yessss. I'm not a baby!" Ann responded huffily.

"I'm not a baaaby!" I mimicked in a whiny voice, then yelped when Ann kicked me in the shin. I gave her a kick right back.

"You are BOTH being baby right now!" Mom shouted, steering with one hand and running a lint roller over her jacket with the other.

Being baby?! Ann and I cracked up and were still laughing when we pulled up in front of Thomas Jefferson Middle School.

Ann took a deep breath and opened the door. Before she got out, I felt a moment of anxiety for her. How did Ann become a middle schooler so fast? I hope she fared better on her first day than I did. On mine, I wore the same T-shirt as a popular girl who loudly pointed out that I wasn't wearing a bra yet. Yeah, no duh. WHY would I need to wear a bra when my chest looked like a Ken doll's? Joke's on you! Ha-ha!

Ann looked like a little kid as she stood outside before shutting the car door. The school yard was already filled with students running around and shouting loudly. She turned back one last time and called out, "Bye!" then walked cautiously toward the front lawn.

I swore I heard my mom sniffle — and was reminded yet again that my sister was, and always would be, the baby of the family. Me on the other hand . . .

"How many honors classes are you taking this year?"

I rolled my eyes. "None. I've been demoted to all reme-dial classes. Actually, they're sending me back to freshman year because of how stupid I am."

"Well, maybe in math, but not in the others."

I stifled a laugh. My mom annoyed me pretty much all the time, but sometimes she revealed a surprising sense of humor, even when she wasn't trying to be funny.

"I'm taking honors English, history, and biology." Ugh.

She nodded, satisfied. "Okay, work hard this year." If I rolled my eyes back any farther they would plop like Ping-Pong balls into my spine.

We pulled up to the front of Bay High, and a gaggle of girls in butt-hugging denim skirts and Ugg boots walked by.

I shuddered inwardly. I guess some still showed up in their fall finest.

"Bye, Mom!" I grabbed my backpack and quickly crawled out of the car before she could ask any more questions.

"Be good!" she yelled as I walked as rapidly away from the car as possible. Honestly, "Be good"? Sometimes I won-dered what in the world my mom thought my life was like when I went to school — did she think I suddenly grew tattoos on my lower back and beat up small children? Seriously. Little did she know how pathetically good I really was. No need to share that shame with my own mother, however.

I was swallowed up by a sea of students as I entered the campus. Our school was basically a brick prison surround-ing a giant courtyard we called the Quad (or the Courtyard

4

O' Judgment). Because we have perfect weather all year round in San Diego, the school forced us to socialize outdoors, squeezing us into the Quad. I walked into the middle of the concrete abyss and squinted as I looked around for three familiar faces.

I saw the usual group of impeccably dressed girls with their giant brand-name handbags that weighed more than they did. Then there was the Asian Christian crowd who laughed uproariously at something or other. They eyed me warily, not knowing what to make of the Korean girl who didn't listen to K-pop or go to church. The Mexican Americans made up the second largest minority group at Bay and were also über hipsters. So many fixed-gear bikes and tight jeans, it ain't even funny.

The obligatory group of nerds took up a small space in a corner, their laptops out — undoubtedly playing video games or dismantling governments. Most of them were boys, boys who were all either abnormally small or large and wearing ironic T-shirts. Weirdly enough, the jocks took up real estate right next to the nerds. They were the loudest bunch, of course, obnoxiously throwing their heads back with laughter, wrestling each other, screeching "Are you *serious*?!" — making their presence felt and heard from every nook and cranny of the campus.

And where did I fit in to this delightful mixed bag of high school stereotypes? In a strange land called My Friends. We were content with each other, and honestly, we had floated through freshman year happily off the radar. We had managed to avoid any real contact with the loathsome popular crowd, but at the same time didn't delve into the nerd realm either.

I thought of my lackluster freshman year. The school was huge and daunting, the classes hard, and there were way too many annoying people for comfort. I put in minimal effort with any extracurriculars and kept to myself. In other words, I was a nobody, and kept my head down hoping that no one would ever notice me. My only joy came in the form of my three best friends.

"Hey!"

I spun around to see David rolling up on his trusty skateboard. Tall and lanky (I swear he grew a foot over the summer), he wore a knit beanie pulled over his mop of brown hair and a pair of Ray Bans.

"Wow. Uh, nice shades," I said.

He grinned. "I'm trying out a new look. I'm hoping it'll discourage people from talking to me this year. Do I look standoffish?"

"No, you look douche-offish."

He threw his head back in an exaggerated laugh, slapping his knee and everything. I pushed him in response.

"*Anyway.* Why are you here so early?" I asked. David was always late to school, and yet he still managed straight As. Damn slacker overachiever!

"First day of school and all. Also, my dad made me by threatening me with weekend school again."

I snickered. "Despite your veneer of coolness, you're still a Chinese kid."

"HALF Chinese, thank you very much."

"That half will always overrule the Irish half." David's mom was Irish, while his dad was second-generation Chinese. His parents were way cooler than mine.

David yawned. "Well, I AM really good at math. Speaking of, are you in Fifth Grade Long Division this year?"

I laughed despite the insult. It's true, math wasn't exactly my forte. Whatever the opposite of forte was, that's what math was to me.

"NO. Remedial Third Grade Multiplication Tables, actually. Hey, what art classes are you taking?" Maddeningly, David was not only good at boring things like math, but fun things like art, too. In fact, I considered him to be a pretty good artist, although no way in hell would I ever tell him.

David instantly perked up. "Oh yeah! I *finally* got into Art II this year. Can you believe they're letting me do *actual* art now?"

I was genuinely happy for him. "Awesome! Yeah, that was really lame, making you take all those exploratory classes last year. At least we got to take that one color wheel class together. I mean, we really excelled at making color wheels."

Just then Elizabeth trotted up to us, Starbucks cup in hand. "It's way too early for you guys to be all *The Holly and David Show* already."

I looked at her long legs in slim jeans tucked into gleaming riding boots, her cashmere scarf, and her perfectly straightened dark hair. "My mom would gladly kill me to have you as her daughter instead, Liz."

She took off her Prada sunglasses, looked me up and down, and tsked. "And who could blame her? Seriously, Holly? A sweatshirt? What happened to the cute leggings outfit I planned for you?"

"I let Ann wear it."

Liz shook her head. "Please. Why do I even bother?"

"Are you drinking coffee? What are you, thirty?" I asked incredulously.

She made a face. "Ugh, and ruin my teeth? No, it's a nonfat milk matcha green tea."

David and I were silent for a second before cracking up. "Matcha WHAT?" David managed to blurt out.

"It's a type of green tea that you whip . . . never mind! Why do I even bother with you cretins?" she asked, trying to keep a smile off her face. David and I lived to torment Liz, who couldn't stand anything icky and uncouth. In other words, us. I liked to think of us as emissaries of reality to Liz, who kind of lived in a Persian princess bubble.

"So, Holly, I have a really cool extracurricular activity to add to your super busy schedule this year," Liz said with excitement.

I looked at her suspiciously. "What?"

"Ballet!" she said with a graceful plié.

I snorted. "HA! Good one."

She shrugged. "It was worth a try. My mom is on a rampage to get me to start dancing again. She says I need another activity to put on my future college application."

"Ugh, don't remind me," I grumbled. "My parents gave

me a huge lecture this summer about taking my studies 'seriously' now that it's sophomore year. Like, yeah, up to this point I thought studying was just a fun little side activity I did every day of my life."

"I love how our parents think we have to be reminded about why we go to school," David said. "Oh, study? Right, right."

We were walking over to an empty lunch table when Carrie sprinted up to us. Her long reddish-blond hair flapped behind her as she just missed a collision with a group of people. Had to love Carrie. She's been one of my best friends for ten years, which is practically the entire time I've been conscious. She's always been an energetic ball of klutziness trapped inside a petite athletic build.

She joined us and in one motion wedged an apple in her mouth, waved to us excitedly, took a huge bite, and managed to blurt out, "Oh my God, Ted Levy looks so cute this year. Have you seen him?"

"Noooo," David replied in a high voice.

Carrie punched him in the shoulder. "Not you. Man, he got hot over the summer. Grew like three inches."

Liz made a face while taking a sip of her matcha latte, or whatever the heck it was. "I doubt a few measly inches made him that much cuter. No one at this school is even *remotely* hot," she said with typical Liz disdain. When people first meet her, they often think she's a snob. I can't argue with that, though, because she kind of is. It's one of the many reasons we get along.

Carrie hooted and chunks of apple flew out of her mouth. "You are so picky. You've got to face reality — a young Clive Owen doesn't exist in all of San Diego, especially not at stupid BHS."

Liz sighed. "You should never give up on your dreams."

David made a barfing noise, then hopped back onto his board. "And on that note, I'm out. See you dorks later!" He zipped off just as the bell rang. The entire campus seemed to groan collectively.

Carrie, Liz, and I looked at each other, a familiar sadness descending. Summer was really over, and our sophomore year had officially begun.

"Well, here we go again." I sighed and shifted my backpack. "I hope it's not boring this year."

"I hope Ted's in one of my classes this year!" Carrie squealed.

"I hope I get through this year without seeing either of you in sweatpants," Liz announced, putting her sunglasses back on.

"Here's the first finished article of the year!"

A piece of paper fluttered down onto my desk.

Isabel Morales, the no-nonsense editor-in-chief of *The Weasel Times*, had just handed me the first article I would copyedit for the school paper. Tall, athletic, and always dressed in a haphazard too-busy-to-fuss-over-clothes manner, Isabel was an intimidating but down-to-earth boss.

"Cool." I picked it up with my red pen in hand, poised to shred it to grammatically correct pieces.

This was my first year as a staff member of *The Weasel Times*, assigned to the post of copy editor, or glorified mistake-fixer. (Yes, *The Weasel Times*. Yes, our school mascot is a weasel. Yes, the school founders were apparently a bunch of masochists. Or maybe weasels were really in during the 1940s.)

I had spent the first few days of my journalism period being bored to tears while watching everyone else work on their stories, so I picked up the article with relish.

Someone's rattling cough startled me, and I glanced to my right at the guy who would handle my edits. Ryder Yates was the designer who laid out all the pages and flowed all the text once I was finished with it. He was also the biggest stoner ever. In fact, he probably didn't even know what class he was in right now.

After I read the first few sentences of the article, I was already bored. It was a column written by a senior named Stephanie Gonzales, all about how excited she was for the upcoming school year.

"Kill me," I muttered as I fixed typos, incorrect spelling, and misuses of semicolons. Fifteen minutes later, I was finished. My, how time flies when life sucks.

I looked around the room and stifled a yawn. I glanced at my computer screen. Forty minutes of class to go. Good God.

I needed to kill some time. I looked through the newspaper's folders on my computer. Sure enough, there was Stephanie's lame excuse for a column. It wouldn't be half bad with a few adjustments. I printed out a fresh copy, got out my red pen again, and made a few tiny changes:

NEW BEGINNINGS, ~~NEW HOPES~~ *MORE OF THE SAME CRAP*

By ~~Stephanie Gonzales~~ Holly Kim

Another school year has begun, and you can feel the ~~excitement~~ *hormones* here at Bay High.

I, for one, am looking forward to growing a year ~~wiser~~ *dumber* through my ~~advanced placement~~ *abysmal California public school education.* ~~classes~~—if there's one thing my immigrant parents taught me, it's to never ~~take your~~ *have fun* ~~education for granted.~~ And I'm proud to say that I've ~~worked hard for~~ *half-assed* the past ~~three~~ years to be where I am today: a ~~senior getting ready to apply to some top-notch~~ *sophomore who's counting the days until graduation* ~~colleges.~~

There are so many things to look forward to this year: ~~Seeing old friends and making~~ *Mocking the jocks. Picking on band geeks. Throwing trash on the dance team* ~~new ones. Going to football games on cool autumnal nights. The excitement at pep~~ *during pep rallies* ~~rallies. Making new discoveries in classes~~—the possibilities are endless!

As I enter my ~~senior~~ *sophomore* year, I can only look back on the past ~~three~~ years with ~~fondness~~ *boredom* and heartfelt ~~nostalgia~~ *irritation*. My years at BHS ~~have~~ *has* been filled with friends, laughter, and a real sense of ~~community~~ *disdain*. I will ~~cherish~~ *forget* my years here, forever. *at the expense of others*

Freshmen, my advice to you is this: Enter the doors every morning with ~~an open mind~~ *pure terror* ~~and happiness~~—you'll find ~~yourself learning so much and forging valuable friendships.~~ *enemies around every corner*

Sophomores: ~~Take what you have learned that tough first year, and make yourself grow as both a student and human being.~~ *We still suck, but at least we're not Freshmen*

Juniors: With SATs around the corner, ~~this will undoubtedly be a challenging year~~—but ~~it will also be the most rewarding.~~ *at least the end is near* Surround yourself with ~~positivity~~ *negativity* and you can ~~accomplish anything!~~ *fail miserably* *because it's all downhill from here. How sad that, for some of you, this is the best it will ever get.*

And, finally, ~~fellow~~ Seniors: Have the time of your lives.

~~Signing off,~~ *See ya. wouldn't want to be ya,* ~~Steph~~ *Holly*

I giggled as I signed my name with a flourish. How amazing would Stephanie Gonzales be if she wrote that?

The bell rang. Thank God. I shoved my fake article into my backpack and tossed the copyedited column into Stoner Yates's folder as I flew out the door. Maybe journalism wouldn't be too bad after all.

TWO

. . . .

SAN DIEGO TEEN'S STUPID STUNT
SENDS FAMILY TO EARLY GRAVE

*S*wish, *swish, swish.*

I loved the sound of the wind whipping past my ears when I zoomed through town on my bike.

Because I'm fifteen, I could technically get my driving permit now. But to be honest, I preferred to ride my bike all over San Diego. It was one of the few times when I felt totally in control and at peace, and one of the only things I was allowed to do without my parents having a total freak-out.

I lived in Pacific Beach and was headed home. I was considering swinging by Carrie's place (she lives like four blocks away from me), when I felt my cell phone vibrate in my pocket.

14

Looking down at the screen, I saw a number that I didn't recognize.

"Hello?" I answered suspiciously, pulling off to the side of the road.

"Is this Holly?" a female voice demanded.

"Um, yes. Who is this?"

"It's Isabel."

"Oh! Hey, Izzie."

"Holly, we've got a huge problem. I just got the first batch of the new issue in —"

"Oh man, did I miss a typo?" I asked, dismayed.

"No, you did not miss a typo! You published a column!"

"Huh? What are you talking about?"

"I'm talking about Stephanie's column that you replaced with your own. You are in such huge trouble, I can't even tell you!"

My heart skipped a beat and I felt light-headed. There was no way. . . .

"Holly, do you hear me? This is serious."

I could barely squeak out, "There's been a mistake. That wasn't a real article — I was just playing around."

"Just playing around?!" Her voice screeched so loudly that I had to move the phone away from my ear. "Good job, genius! It's been published! It's already been sent to all the homerooms for distribution!"

I slowly slid off my bike. "Oh crap!"

"YES! 'Oh crap' is RIGHT!"

My breathing sped up. "Oh crap, oh crap. What am I going to do?"

"I don't know! Your column was so offensive that I'm sure the entire newspaper's going to get hell for this! We're all screwed!"

My life flashed before my eyes. I envisioned my immediate expulsion. I saw my parents breaking down into hysterics. My mother would be wearing one of those white headbands tied around her head — what Koreans wear at funerals when they're throwing themselves onto the floor in front of a picture of the deceased — screaming and crying over my demise. Because really, at that moment, I would be dead to her.

"What can I do? Can't I just explain that it was a mistake?"

Isabel sighed. "I guess. I'm just expecting the worst. We'll see what happens on Monday."

It was Sunday. Just enough time to hop the border and assume a new identity.

"You don't know how to do it, Holly. *Aigo*, just move!"

I moved aside so that the pushy dictator who was my mother could finish making the dumplings. We were prepping a huge meal for yet another family gathering at my house, and yet again my mother was admonishing me in Korean for my lack of dumpling-making expertise.

"Oh, please, holy queen of dumplings, *do* show me the proper way."

She threw me a Mom Glare that had grown increasingly popular lately. A look that said, "I'm not sure what the hell you're actually saying, but I know I don't like it and you need to shut your mouth."

She grabbed the dumpling from me. "You are putting way too much stuffing in here." She scooped some of the raw ground pork from the round dumpling skin and flung it back into the bowl.

"YOU said one spoonful!" I said accusingly.

"Can't you just stand there and say, 'Yes, Mother,' for once? You always have to talk back!" she snapped, carefully closing up the dumpling by dotting the edges with some warm water mixed with egg whites.

"I'm just defending myself. YOU'RE the one who chooses to interpret it as 'talking back.'" I refrained from calling her a fascist.

"There you go again! Forget it, go play with your cousins. You're not helping anyone in here."

"Fine by me!" I huffed and stalked away. I was so annoyed that I didn't even have the energy to make fun of my mom for telling me to go "play" at the age of fifteen. I walked through the living room, which was already crowded with my uncles lounging in front of the TV watching ESPN.

"Holly, why are you out here doing nothing? Try to be helpful sometimes!" one of my more charming uncles bellowed as he sipped his beer. He hadn't moved in two hours. I threw him a dirty look, which made everyone laugh.

Because our extended family usually met for dinner every week, this was the norm. My aunts were in the kitchen fussing over dinner, and my cousins were scattered around the house trying to stave off boredom. Some of the boy cousins were playing video games in the family room, and they yelled at me when I walked in front of the TV. "Oh, get OVER it," I spat, bonking my littlest cousin, Mark, on the head for good measure.

I poked my head into Ann's room to see her and the girl cousins sitting around looking at magazines and staring into laptops. "What are you guys doing?" I asked. They all kind of grunted in response.

What happened to us? We used to talk to each other so much our moms had to tell us to be quiet, that we sounded like a bunch of squawking birds. Now we mostly passed the time in silence, staring into our phones and checking Facebook for the billionth time. "WOW, don't let it get too CUH-RAZY in here!" I said before leaving.

But really — did we have to hang out with everyone every weekend of our lives? I envied Carrie, whose extended family lived scattered across the country. Her weekends consisted of going to the movies with her parents and "Ice Cream Sundae Sunday!" nights. Given the current climate of my impending social and academic suicide, I was so not in the mood for all of this.

I was about to hole up in my room and call Carrie when my mom hollered for me. "Holly! Set the table!" Dinner was ready.

I dragged myself to the dining room, which seated:

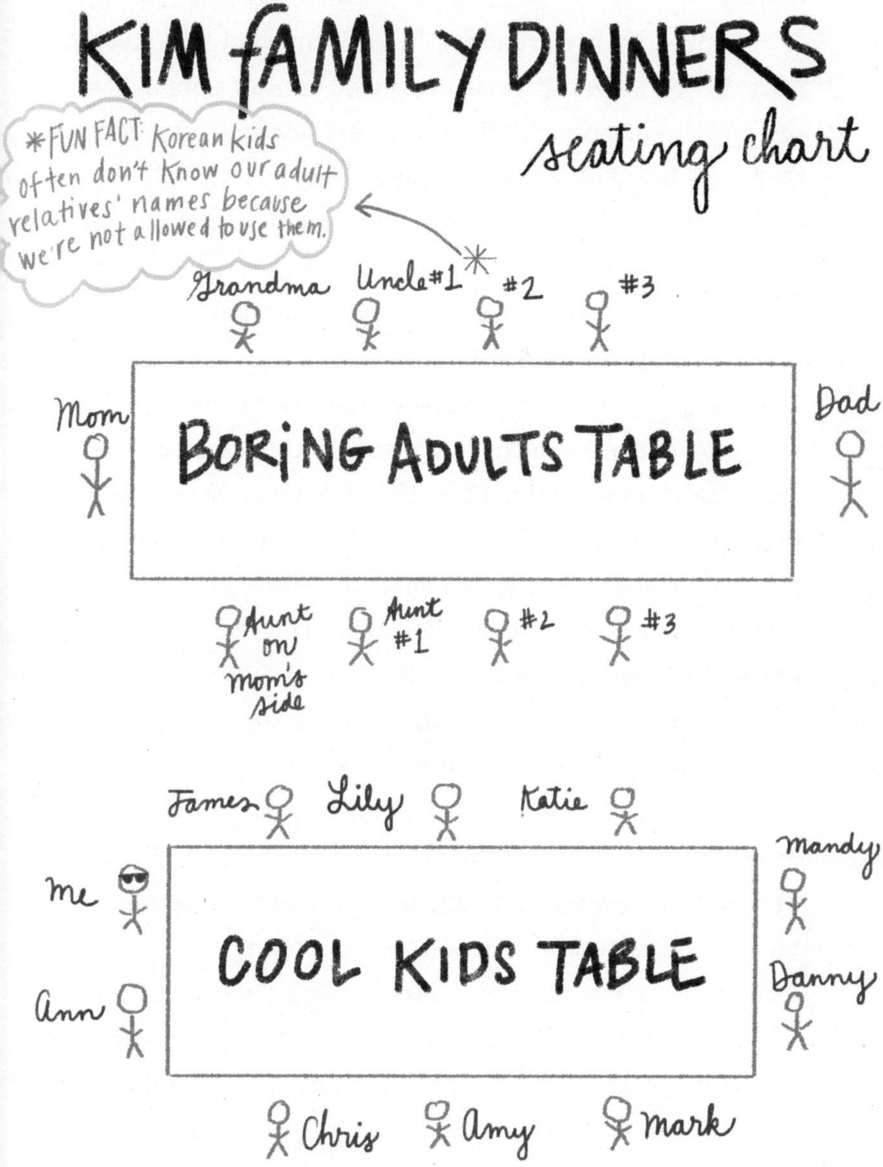
KIM FAMILY DINNERS
seating chart
*FUN FACT: Korean kids often don't know our adult relatives' names because we're not allowed to use them.
Grandma
Uncle #1*
#2
#3
Mom
BORING ADULTS TABLE
Dad
Aunt on mom's side
Aunt #1
#2
#3
James
Lily
Katie
Me
COOL KIDS TABLE
Mandy
Ann
Danny
Chris
Amy
Mark

Yup, twenty people. And that wasn't even my whole family.

I walked by my grandma as she inspected the silverware, her Swarovski crystal–encrusted bifocals perched on the end of her nose. "Holly, this is not good quality. Your mother is being cheap, like always."

I rolled my eyes. "Sorry it's not as good as the queen's silverware, *Halmoni*."

My grandma, or *halmoni*, tsked. "It is just not dignified to have cheap silverware. So common."

I don't know where she gets these airs. As long as I've known her — which is my entire life, I guess — my grandma's carried herself like British royalty. She owns a mahogany four-poster bed in her old folks' home, wears Ferragamo heels, and sports pristine white gloves while driving. A modern-day Grace Kelly living in a senior citizen home in Clairemont Mesa.

"Also, what did I tell you about your hair?"

I reflexively lifted a hand to my choppy, cropped hair. "It won't grow. I must have a terrible disease."

She shook her head with an exasperated frown. It must be tragic to have a granddaughter who doesn't take horseback-riding lessons and refuses to grow long, lovely lady locks. (Yes, horseback-riding lessons. She also hoped that I'd become a tennis champion. I think somewhere along the way my grandmother got confused and thought we were the Korean Kennedys.)

My dad walked up and dropped a platter full of beef on the table. "This is good meat!"

20

How was he the offspring of my grandma? They couldn't be more different. Case in point: the pants he was wearing. They had a hole in the butt and were at least eight years old. If my dad didn't have a family, I'm pretty sure he would have been quite content as a hobo.

Everyone started trickling into the dining room, and I sat down at the kids' table and dug into the food — some grilled short ribs, sautéed spinach and bean sprouts, rice, and a dozen varieties of kimchi. Unlike most Korean dads, my dad did most of the cooking in our household and was really pretty darn good at it. As we sat there chattering and eating, I overheard one of my aunts discussing so-and-so's kid's SAT score.

"She got a 2280. After only one try!"

A murmur of approval went through the entire table. My cousins and I all rolled our eyes and made gagging noises. It was starting — the weekly critique! The lovely portion of the evening where all the parents sat around complaining about their children and comparing them to so-and-so's children.

"Yeah, a 2280 on her SAT. It'll probably set her apart from the million other Asian kids applying to Yale," I said.

Everyone snickered. "But how else will she meet her future Korean financial consultant husband if she doesn't go to Yale?" Amy asked sarcastically — she was about to take the SAT in a few months.

We all laughed while our parents went on with their conversation. My cousins and I had endured each other's company every weekend of our lives, and therefore we were as close as siblings. Except that unlike siblings, we didn't see each other every day, so we didn't hate each other as much.

While digging into my ribs I heard my mom say from the other end of the table, "I worry about how Holly will do on the SAT — she's not the best tester."

Not the best tester? Where was my mom getting these things? And why was she talking like Dr. Phil? Also, the SAT was still a year away! Get a life!

"Um, Mom? I CAN HEAR YOU," I barked across the table.

My aunts and uncles cringed and gave me disapproving looks. Another annoying thing about having aunts and uncles around all the time? They're just a few more parents watching your every move — extra pairs of critiquing eyes.

Can you even imagine these people once I got expelled from school because of my column? My mom would be moaning and pounding her chest at the table, and my aunts and uncles would be trying to console her. Then I'd show up, thirty years old and still trying to graduate high school, pumping my fist in the air and saying, "I got a 2280 on my SAT!"

My mom's eerily calm voice broke my reverie. "Holly, lower your voice." Her eyes betrayed her fury, though. Eek.

There is nothing like the Korean Mom Death Stare. I instantly shrank into my seat, but I also felt a flash of stubborn rebellion. I was so sick of feeling like I was getting in trouble all the damn time. I gave her a look in return, which startled her momentarily, and I wondered if I would be dying tonight.

While everyone was still eating, I slipped out into the backyard where my dad was grilling on the barbeque.

"Do you want more chicken?" he asked as he tossed some meat onto the grill.

It smelled delicious, so I nodded.

"Okay, then."

It was nice and quiet outside, and I was grateful for how simple my relationship with my dad was. He was content feeding me chicken, and I was content eating it.

While my mom and I butted heads constantly, my dad understood me in a way my mom didn't. He and my mother were so different — she, anxious and quick tempered, and he, all Zen Buddha. In the immortal words of Paula Abdul, I guess opposites *do* attract.

"Can I also have some pork?" I asked. He slid some delicious grilled pork belly onto my plate.

We sat there in silence for a little while as I watched my dad lay strips of meat on the grill methodically and slowly, how he approached everything in life. The column incident had been in the back of my mind all evening, and it killed me that I somehow couldn't bring it up with my dad. It had been years since I talked to my parents about anything remotely personal. Once I hit puberty, it was Awkwardville. I had crossed some line and couldn't go back.

"Thanks for the food."

He grunted, his attention on the grill.

So instead of pouring out my feelings to my dad with cheesy music playing in the background á la Happy Sitcom

Family, I shuffled to my room and tried to ease the panic rising in me.

Would anyone even care about the article? Was I making a huge deal out of something that could potentially slip under the radar? How would I convince everyone that it was a joke?

Hours later, after the tea had been served and everyone started dozing off into food comas, my relatives finally left and my family got ready for bed. Needless to say, I didn't get any sleep that night. I tossed and turned with an endless list of excuses in my head and felt both terror and relief shoot through me as daylight peeked through my window.

Here we go.

THREE

· ·

TOP TEN UNCONVENTIONAL WAYS
TO GAIN POPULARITY!

You are my hero."

I shut my locker to see David holding up the latest issue of *The Weasel Times*.

He was laughing.

"This is *not* funny, D." I snatched the paper out of his hands.

"Come on, it's funny. Nobody knew who you were yesterday, and now you're *famous*!"

"But I don't *want* to be famous!" I whined.

David leaned against the lockers. "Why didn't you tell me about this, anyway? If I'd known I was going to start Monday with this awesome piece of high-quality journalism, I would have actually been on time for homeroom."

At that moment, a beautiful senior girl three bra sizes larger than me walked by and muttered, "Bitch."

My mouth dropped open and I looked at David. "Did you hear that?" I hissed.

A flash of anger crossed his face, but then he waved his hand dismissively. "Typical, low-life lemming behavior. Don't sweat it."

I felt a lump in my throat as I watched the senior walk away nonchalantly. Then I looked around at everyone hanging out by their lockers for other signs of hostility. It was almost second period, so at this point I was guessing a lot of people had seen my column already. *The Weasel Times* was really popular, and we were always eager to do anything but listen to announcements during homeroom.

Carrie came running toward me at breakneck speed, clutching a copy of the newspaper to her chest. She stopped and leaned over for a second, out of breath, before panting, "Oh my God, tell me this is a joke?"

I bit my lip and wanted to die for the hundredth time that day. "Well. It was a mistake."

Swatting her sweat-dampened hair out of her eyes, Carrie stared at me long and hard. "What do you mean, a mistake? People are going to kill you for this. Like, seriously kill you. Like, they are going to throw stuff at you and then like, beat you, and then, like —"

"I GET IT. See, I copyedited this other column by Stephanie Gonzales, but I did it as a joke and I must have submitted the wrong version to our stupid stoner designer. . . ." I trailed off.

"So has anyone tried to kill you yet?" Carrie asked, looking a little worried.

"No. But the day is young. Also, this senior girl just called me a bitch."

Carrie's face turned bright red and she whipped her head around, eyes blazing. "WHO? She better show her damn face and know who she's dealing with!"

She may be the daughter of two tree-hugging hippies, but Carrie has one mean temper if provoked. Once, in third grade, she pushed a boy off a swing because he was hogging it. And in eighth grade she was suspended one day for kicking a girl who had pushed Liz into the grass during PE.

"Thanks, but if you try to beat up everyone who hates me today . . . well, I dunno. You'd be tired."

I feebly said good-bye to David and Carrie and walked to my history class, where Liz was waiting, holding the paper gingerly in her hands.

Silence.

"I know," I said wearily.

"You should hire me to do your PR. How else do you expect to survive high school?"

At the beginning of class I dodged a few dirty looks. But what's weird is that I also got the vibe that some people were actually being nice to me. Was there something sinister lurking behind their smiles? Or could they have possibly liked my accidental column?

A girl sitting to my left, who had never said two words to me before, leaned over and said, "Sweet piece in the paper. The funniest thing ever!"

I blinked and shook my head quickly, like a dog.

"Seriously?!" I whispered furtively.

Before she could answer, I was shushed loudly by this goody two-shoes named Caroline, who was sitting to my right. I made a face at her and snapped my head back to attention.

I tried to keep my mind on the history lesson — something about the French Revolution. Man, those revolutionaries were brutal. I mean, who *doesn't* hate rich people who eat cake all day? But head chopping was taking it a little too far, in my opinion. Anyway.

My thoughts wandered back to my accidental column, and I snuck a glance at the girl on my left. (I didn't even know her name!)

Hm, a fan. Something I did not anticipate.

A few minutes into Mr. Reilly's lesson, someone walked into the class and handed him a note. Everyone started murmuring excitedly in that way high school kids do when there is even the slightest distraction.

After reading the note, Mr. Reilly looked straight up at me. My mouth got very dry.

"Holly? Can you come up here please?"

I tried walking up there all casual-like, ignoring the whispering masses.

Mr. Reilly leaned in toward me and said in a low voice, "You need to see the guidance counselor Mrs. Karkis right now. Just take this pass to her office."

I tried to remain calm. "Um, why?"

Mr. Reilly raised his eyebrows as if to say, "Like you don't know."

I shuffled back to my desk to grab my things. I tried to coolly stuff my binder and pencil case into my backpack, but dropped the tin case onto the floor, making a huge clattering noise. All heads spun in my direction and a few people snickered. Ugh.

I finally fled the room, but not without one of the belt loops on my jeans getting caught on the door handle. Seriously?

AHHHH!

Take a deep breath.

I got to Mrs. Karkis's office and knocked on the door.

"Come in."

I stepped in and noticed someone else sitting in a chair in the corner. It was Mr. Williams, the journalism advisor. "Oh, Lord," I thought to myself. It *was* about the column. But why was I being called into the guidance counselor's office of all places?

I only ever saw Mr. Williams in brief glimpses during my journalism period. He usually hung out in his office and politely ignored everyone. Now I would probably get an earful.

"Please take a seat, Holly." Mrs. Karkis motioned toward a chair. I sat down nervously. The only other time I'd ever been in her office was to change my class schedule last year, when she thought it was a great idea for me to take a woodshop class instead of art. She thought I needed to "expand" my interests. Okay yeah, hanging out with male thugs every fifth period, a billion miles away from the rest of the campus in some godforsaken warehouse by the football field? No thanks. After my third trip to her office, she finally let me take the art class.

"Holly, what were you thinking when you wrote that column?" she asked, hands folded primly on her desk.

"I wasn't thinking. I mean, it wasn't meant to be published! It was a joke—"

"A JOKE?" Mrs. Karkis sputtered.

"I didn't think anyone would read it.... I was just being ... ridiculous? I mean, I don't *really* hate everyone that much...." I trailed off lamely. Everything I said sounded like an excuse from a creepy future school shooter.

Mr. Williams made a funny noise from his corner that I could have sworn was a snicker. Men of all ages have mastered the fine art of snickering.

Mrs. Karkis sighed and went on. "Well, thanks to your 'joke,' you have offended almost every single person at this school. As well as the administration."

I tried to swallow the lump in my throat. "So what's going to happen to me?"

Mrs. Karkis sighed, took off her glasses, and said in a gentler tone, "My concern is: Why so hostile? What's going on in"—she pointed at her chest—"here?"

I didn't even know what to say, I was so embarrassed for both of us.

"Um. I-I'm not *really* hostile," I said in a small voice. A snort of laughter again from Mr. Williams.

"I'm not! I mean, I just—I'm a normal teenage kid, right? Angst and all that? It's not like I'm going to shoot up the school or anything...."

Mrs. Karkis's eyebrows shot up dangerously. "Don't even joke about that!" she hissed.

I was baffled. Why was she asking me this stuff? Wasn't it clear that I wasn't really that psycho? The column wasn't meant to be seen by anyone! And then I got uncomfortable — maybe everyone else at school actually thought I was nuts, too. Oh, God, why couldn't I just have left well enough alone and stayed invisible?

Suddenly distracted by a small *bleep!* from her computer, Mrs. Karkis tried to talk to me while clicking around with her mouse. "Well, Holly. People are offended. And you really should be more aware of people's feelings. And of your own as well, sweetie."

What the — ?! Was I actually in a guidance counselor's office to be guided and counseled? Unheard of! I thought all these people did was mess with our class schedules and then call it a day.

"Okaaay. Is that it? I'm not in trouble? Should I write some kind of retraction or something?"

I looked at Mrs. Karkis expectantly, but she was distracted by what I could have sworn was a Tumblr blog featuring cats wearing fedoras. Once again, I was truly impressed by the intellectual brains that ran my school.

Mr. Williams cleared his throat and moved his chair over to me. "Hi, Holly. Actually, I had something more than a retraction in mind. But before we go into that, you do realize that what you did was really, really stupid, right?"

I looked down at my lap. "Yes."

31

"And you do know that *The Weasel Times* has yet another controversy on its hands?"

It was true. The paper was constantly berated by the school administration. Like last year, when they ran an article about the student government's corruption in assigning student parking spaces. I thought it was a fine piece of investigative journalism, but apparently the student government members got pretty pissed and demanded that the principal stop funds for the newspaper. Babies.

Mr. Williams leaned back, crossed his arms, and said in a slow, deliberate voice, "But we welcome controversy."

Huh?

"This may be a huge mistake, but my instincts are telling me that you have — uh — a way with words."

I was so confused!

"What are you getting at?" I asked impatiently.

He raised an eyebrow with amusement. "Yeah, quite the mouth on this one. I think you'd make an excellent columnist."

"Huh?!"

"Would you want to write a real column for *The Weasel Times?*"

"Are you for real?"

"Yes, I'm for real."

"For real, for real?"

"Holly!"

"Okay, okay. Just making sure. I mean, because I don't know if anyone's going to want to read my column. Everyone is probably freaking out," I said.

"Yeah, some uptight teachers and students are, but a lot of them are also laughing."

Mrs. Karkis glared at both of us. "One needn't be considered *uptight* to be offended. It was offensive. And the only reason the administration is going along with this is because I convinced them that maybe this would be therapeutic for you and your anger issues."

I tried to hold back a giggle. "I don't have any anger issues."

This time both Mr. Williams and Mrs. Karkis laughed. I looked between them defensively.

Mr. Williams shook his head and said, "The thing is, you got a reaction out of people. What's important is not whether your opinion is popular, it's that people react to what you write. *The Weasel Times* has never been too concerned with popularity anyhow," he added.

Interesting. Did I really want to trade in my blissful anonymity for the drama I had endured today? But if I didn't do anything about it, say anything about it, all people would remember me by was that column. Which, while funny to some, was probably not the best representation of me.

I thought about the impending school year stretched out before me: the daily monotonous routine of getting through classes, with my friends as the only bright spot of my high school existence.

I thought of people actually reading what I had to say. And me, having a proper outlet for my opinions.

I took a deep breath and smiled.

"Okay. Sign me up, dudes."

LETTERS TO THE EDITOR

What genius gave Holly Kim her own column? I will no longer read this crappy paper. I only read it for the two measly comics you guys put in there anyways.

SEE ya.

— MIKE J., SOPHOMORE

I think it's totally rude of you guys to give Holly her own column after that totally offensive article she wrote. She obviously doesn't respect us. Why should we be forced to open the school paper and be judged by her every week? Um, also? NO ONE asked.

— ANONYMOUS, JUNIOR

This is for Holly: YOU RULE! I hate BHS, too! We suck.

Rock on,

— VLADIMIR P., FRESHMAN

Why is everyone at this school so sensitive anyway? Do you not know how annoying you all are??? Seriously, get over yourselves. Don't let people get you down, Holly. I can't wait to read your column every month!

— KAREN S., SOPHOMORE

Who cares about this column thing by that loser Holly? Why aren't you guys concentrating more on the football season? BHS is going to KICK ASS this year. WOO!

— TREVOR F., SENIOR

OCTOBER

Oh, the sweet smell of Homecoming. And by "sweet" I mean retching.

In theory, I like Homecoming. I like how it falls in . . . the fall. I love the idea of traditional — and slightly lame — high school rivalry dating back to the days when high school kids wore sweaters with letters on them.

I like how the Homecoming game got its name from all the alumni, young and old, coming back home to root for their alma mater on a crisp, autumn evening — or as crisp as it can get in San Diego. (Why is it that all seasonal stereotypes assume everyone lives in New England? States like California were founded like a hundred years ago. Time to get with this century.)

Anyway. I like watching kids get manic about who's taking whom to the dance. I like how during Homecoming week we get to do weird things like wear our pajamas to show school spirit. I like how at the rally, we all get to smash apart a Volkswagen Bug painted orange to show our aggression for our rivals, the Kennedy Tigers.

This year's Homecoming game should be

pretty sweet — I hear Kennedy's football lineup really sucks.

Not that I know anything about football, but last I heard, Kennedy's captain got suspended for selling weed. Classy. And supposedly their quarterback is fat.

I don't say these things out of misguided school pride. It's because I find pleasure in making fun of people outside of our school once in a while. And this seems like a better time than any, right?

As for the Homecoming Court, where shall I begin?

I find the whole idea ridiculous. Yes, I do. As if high school isn't dysfunctional enough, let's throw in a massive popularity contest. And we all know that the male portion of the Homecoming Court isn't judged as critically as the female portion.

Because for the gals, not only do they have to meet the popularity prerequisite, they have to possess beauty-pageant looks as well. Why not just bust out a swimsuit competition and have court hopefuls catwalk in their bikinis during lunch one day? It wouldn't make the Homecoming Court any more sexist than it already is.

So while I enjoy the idea of Homecoming and maybe even the outdated idea of temporary "school spirit," I am 100 percent against voting for a Homecoming Court. Didn't we establish two hundred years ago that America is so not into the idea of monarchies? Our forefathers would be disappointed.

Rah Rah Sis Boom Bah,

Holly

FOUR

· ·

BHS WAITS IN EAGER ANTICIPATION FOR HOMECOMING DANCE LOCATION. REALLY.

The student body president's voice squawked over the speakers. "Yes, you heard correctly, we'll be hosting the Homecoming dance in our very own gym this year! We know we're going to have an AWESOME Homecoming! Go Weasels!"

Everyone around me started grumbling and moaning.

"THE GYM? It's in the *gym*?!"

"Sooo lame!"

"Oh, wah."

Well, that last one was me.

It was lunchtime, and everyone had stopped in their tracks to listen to the latest announcements about this year's Homecoming — gossip had been buzzing for days about where we would hold the dance this year.

Concentrating intensely on balancing my pizza slices and bag of chips, I approached Liz and David at our usual lunch spot under a large oak tree. David was standing precariously on his skateboard, while Liz was perched daintily on a bench wearing a gauzy patterned dress belted at the waist. I looked down at my striped shirt, jeans, and high-top Chucks. I always looked like a twelve-year-old boy next to Liz.

Before I could greet them, two freshmen girls walked by consoling each other, near tears over the announcement. David called out, "Oh my God, who *cares*?!" Their jaws dropped and they hurried away, sniffling petulantly. Ah, we're a friendly bunch.

Liz threw him an incredulous look. "Who cares? David, do you really want to wear a tux that you rented for ninety bucks in the same gross room where tall, sweaty guys play basketball?"

"Uh, no. Because I don't plan on renting a tux. Do you even know me?" David asked while nimbly jumping off his board to sit on the grass in one clean swoop.

I sat down on my backpack next to him (there's nothing worse than wet grass stains on your butt, even if you are just wearing an old pair of jeans) and laughed at Liz's contemptuous glare.

She huffily kicked off her gray suede ballet flats to tuck her feet beneath her. "Okay, well, for some of us, the idea of a school dance in the gym is so lame. They had it at the W Hotel last year!"

Boring. I turned my attention to chowing down my wholesome meal when Carrie jogged up to us, out of breath. She tossed her macramé tote onto the ground dramatically. "Hey, guys. Can you believe Mrs. Worthington held me in class during lunch because she thought I was mocking her Spanish lesson behind her back? I mean, I was, but God, she was using the tiny microphone again. How could I resist? And to deprive me of my lunch! I'm pretty sure that's against the law."

"Wait, you were just *hanging out* with Mrs. Worthington? I always wondered what she made you delinquents do during lunch," Liz mused.

Carrie rolled her eyes and wedged herself between David and me, grass stains be damned in her cut-off shorts. "She literally made me sit at my desk and read my Spanish book for twenty minutes. While she sat at her desk and ate a peanut-butter-and-jelly sandwich. In silence."

"That's sad. I'm too sad to eat my pizza now." I stared mournfully at my meal, working to keep a straight face.

"Don't you remember how insane ol' Worthington used to be in Intro to Spanish? She would almost throw our desks across the room if we didn't address her as *Señora* Worthington."

It's true. The rest of us were one year ahead of Carrie in Spanish (in a lot of subjects actually — Carrie's parents didn't push her to take every honors class in the world), and spent most of last year's class trying not to die laughing.

Liz let out an unladylike snort and said, "That

microphone. I mean, WHY did she need to lecture with a microphone? *We can hear you, Señora. Esta muy fuerte.*"

We all laughed while Carrie looked confused. "What's *fuerte* mean again?"

David threw a straw wrapper at her braided head. "You *deserve* your sad-sack lunchtime with Mrs. Worthington."

Liz kindly removed the wrapper from Carrie's hair. "Well, anyway, all you missed was David's usual antisocial 'cool kid' act. He doesn't want to go to the dance," Liz tattled.

Carrie shrugged. "Well, it's in the gym now, so who cares, right?" She reached over to grab a pizza slice off my plate. This might be considered super rude behavior by, oh, *everyone*, but we've been sharing/stealing each other's food since we were five. I slapped her hand but was too slow, and she held up the slice triumphantly.

Liz groaned. "I *know*. Can you believe the incompetent idiots in the student government decided to do that? I honestly think it's because they ran out of money after buying monogrammed jackets for themselves."

Carrie looked up thoughtfully while nibbling on her ill-gotten pizza slice. "I wonder if I should ask Scott to the dance."

I almost choked. "SCOTT? What happened to the love of your life, Ted?"

"Oh, please," Carrie scoffed, waving her hand dismissively in the air. "That was so last month. I'm in love with Scott now."

Liz wrinkled her nose. "Um, Scott on the water polo team?"

Carrie closed her eyes and murmured, "Yessss."

"Um — *cough* — douche!" David said while pulling his sunglasses on nonchalantly.

"He's NOT a douche! Just because he's a jock doesn't mean he's like, Matthew Reynolds."

We all made faces and said collectively, "Matthew Reynolds. Bleeeugh."

Liz daintily wiped her mouth. "Well, I still think Water Polo Scott is pretty ick."

"WHY?" Carrie said, frustrated. "Just because he isn't fluent in five languages and doesn't look like an Urban Outfitters model?"

"Um, no. Because he hits on any girl within ten feet of him. And also, Urban Outfitters? Please, I'm not Holly," she said disdainfully while applying lip gloss.

I shrugged. "I have a soft spot for boyish hungry types, what can I say?"

Carrie plopped her head into my lap and brought her hand up to her forehead dramatically. "I only *wish* I could be within those ten feet of Scott! He's my future husband, I can *feel* it."

I giggled. "You're crazy. And you're crazy to want to go to the Homecoming dance."

Liz dug into her giant Marc Jacobs bag and whipped out the latest issue of *The Weasel Times* and shook it right in front of my nose. "Speaking of! This month's column was so annoying!"

"What, why?" I asked while swatting Liz's hands away from my face.

"What's your deal with the Homecoming Court? You sound insane!"

"Excuse me?" I replied, slightly offended. "What's 'insane' about it? I think the whole thing is dumb."

David lifted up his sandwich in solidarity. "What up."

Liz looked at all of us and inhaled deeply. "Well, it's a shame you feel that way. Because I'm running for Homecoming Queen."

It was as if she'd announced that she was really a man. Or middle class.

"Are you joking?" I asked.

Throwing me an exasperated look specially patented by Liz herself, she said, "No, I'm not joking."

"Seriously?" David asked. "Why?"

"Yeah, why?" Carrie seconded.

"BECAUSE. I WANT TO."

We stared at her, Carrie's pizza crust hanging in the air.

Not making eye contact with us, she got up abruptly from the bench, shoved her shoes back on, and stomped away.

"Liz! LIIIZ!" Carrie called out. Then she looked at us. "Man, she's for real!"

David shook his head. "She's being so bizarre."

"Yeah, what's with the sudden Homecoming Queen aspirations?" I asked.

Carrie sighed. "I think we need to remember that Liz isn't really a hater, like us. I feel bad."

"Me too," I said.

We looked at David. He shrugged. "Well, I mean — Homecoming QUEEN?"

"But I think she's serious!" I said.

"I know she is, that's what's so scary," said David.

While I sat in journalism after lunch, I thought about Liz's sudden interest in the Homecoming Court. It just didn't make sense.

I first met Liz in middle school — she was the new girl in seventh grade and was instantly taken in by the so-called "popular girls." It's weird, but teen movies get it right with these kinds of girls. They're all perfectly coiffed and bitchy to the max. And they are unbelievably elitist. Ugh, I'm getting irritated just thinking about them.

Anyway, this clique of gals was quick to latch on to Liz because, on the surface, she was an asset for them. Let me explain it this way — when she first walked into my homeroom class, this is what she looked like:

Okay, not really. But the thing is, she was super gorgeous and super well-dressed and groomed. I remember thinking, "Oh, brother."

And it didn't help that there were rumors swirling around school about how rich her family was. Apparently, she had lived in Paris for a few years while her dad ran some kind of bank, and her mother was a former model. At the time, I wondered why they chose to move to San Diego, of all unglamorous places. (I later learned it was because her huge extended Persian family all lived here.)

So imagine my surprise when she approached Carrie and me one day during lunch.

"Hi, my name's Elizabeth. May I sit with you guys?"

I'm sure both our faces looked like this: :O

"Um, yeah!" Carrie sputtered, pushing her hippie horse food aside to make room on the table.

"Thanks!" She sat down and sighed, pushing her sunglasses on top of her head. (Because of her, a bunch of other girls had started wearing sunglasses, too, prompting a "no sunglasses in class" rule.)

"God, I'm so sick of those Barbie dolls," Liz said while opening up her lunch. I don't know what I was more surprised by — her declaration or the artisan bread and cheese spread that she was unpacking.

"You mean Candace and all of them?" I asked.

She nodded her head. "They're so immature. And boring."

Carrie laughed. "I don't believe it!"

Liz looked at her curiously. "Why?"

An awkward silence followed, then I said, "Well, because . . . I mean . . . they really like you."

She rolled her eyes. "Oh yeah, they like the idea of me. I'm like, another Barbie doll for the Barbie doll parade."

I giggled. "Yeah, but they're jealous of you, too."

Frowning at her gourmet cheese, Liz said, "Well, I don't want friends like that."

Carrie threw an arm around her with gusto and declared, "We're not like that! Holly and I are the reject Barbie dolls that never made it out of the factory!"

Now it was Liz's turn to laugh. But I was kind of embarrassed by Carrie's unabashed openness with the glamorous new girl.

It took a few weeks for me to warm up to her. I kept thinking that she must have been put up to this by the other girls. And Liz was someone you had to get used to — she was definitely way more mature than Carrie and me. We had just stopped playing with our My Little Ponies a couple summers ago and felt like giant babies next to Liz, who already wore nail polish and lacy Victoria's Secret bras. She also had this way of talking that made her sound way older — like a lady in a soap opera.

But we soon discovered that she had little patience for all the jerks at school — just like us. And I also learned that she was the only other person who could rival me in the size of her book collection. (Although she was way more of a Tolkien geek than I was — I personally can't stand reading about those dorky hobbits.)

So Liz slowly became close friends with us — right around the same time that David started hanging out with us, too. David and I had been lab partners for dissecting frogs, and we bonded the day he made the first incision into the frog, only to have disgusting yellow liquid squirt in his face. At first wary of hanging out with three girls, he slowly started spending more lunches with us until we became the inseparable foursome you know and love today.

Initially, the Barbie dolls were so miffed by Liz's cold shoulder that they tried to make her miserable by spreading all sorts of mean rumors (one saying that she had a mustache!!! LOL). Liz, however, couldn't care less. Or at least that's what I thought at the time. The rumors eventually faded, and the Barbies gave up trying to ruin her life.

Did she still have something to prove to those girls? Because she would be competing against some of them for Homecoming Queen.

I decided then that we'd have to be supportive of Liz — she had been nothing but the most loyal of friends for the past three years.

Speaking of, the hubbub over Homecoming was in full effect in the journalism room. I guess, in light of the newly revealed Homecoming dance location, there was some gleeful complaining to be had. Nothing riles up the *Weasel Times* staff like boneheaded moves by the student government.

Suddenly, Isabel ran over to me frantically crying, "Holly! Stop everything!"

I stilled my hands over the keyboard. I was playing online Scrabble.

"Why? What's up?"

"You need to cover the Homecoming dance!"

I blinked. "Excuse me?"

"We need someone to cover the dance, and you're that person. We got you two tickets, so you and a date get to go for FREE. Isn't that great?"

I stared at her for a second, then realized she was serious.

"NO, THAT IS NOT GREAT! I don't want to go!"

She looked momentarily startled. "Well, too bad."

To which I uttered the most amazing comeback: "You can't make me."

Isabel placed her hands on her hips and shot me a bossy upperclassman glare. "Yes, I can! You're covering the dance!"

"Why do we even need to cover the dance? It's not like, a freaking G8 Summit!" I shouted. "What could possibly happen there that would be worth reporting?" The rest of the journalism staff was now watching us curiously.

"Holly! Don't question me. We're bashing this dance location and we need a staff member there to add legitimacy to our criticism. I know you don't already have plans to go for fun, like most of the other writers here, so I think you're the best choice to go."

How rude.

"So you're going. End of discussion."

Great, just great. Now I had to go to the stupid dance and find a stupid damn date.

FIVE

. . . .

HOW KOREAN IS YOUR MOTHER?

Ugh, what are we listening to, Mom?"

"Christian music."

"WHY? You don't go to church anymore!"

"You don't have to go to church to listen to this! It's beautiful."

"I want to die."

"Don't be so dramatic. This is my car and we'll listen to my music. Not your loud girls-screaming music."

That's how my mother described Best Coast. Nice.

"Thank God we're almost to the mall. Hallelujah, Mom!" I raised my arms to the sky.

She threw me a warning look as we pulled into the Fashion Valley parking lot. We were at the mall to buy some jeans for me and some kitchen products for her. Luckily, Ann was at a friend's house for the day. Shopping with my sister is like shopping with an overheated beast who will at any moment shred clothing racks with her teeth and start screaming that she wants to go home.

We headed straight to the Gap where I knew my trusty dark-wash, straight-leg jeans could be found. Only the best for this fashionista. As I walked out with shopping bag in hand, I noticed a store with party dresses in its window across the way. Dread filled my stomach. Not only did I not want to think about the dance, but I hadn't brought it up with my mom yet either. This seemed like a better time than most, without the audience of my sister and with witnesses around in case my mom tried to kill me.

"Mom, um, I think I have to buy a dress."

My mom scoffed (the Korean Mom Disdainful Scoff — a key element in the fine Asian art of undermining your children's self-esteem). "A dress? Why would you need a dress?"

Even my mom thought I was a loser. I took a deep breath. "Because I have to go to the Homecoming dance."

"*Mwoya?!*" she said in her native tongue — basically the equivalent of WTF?

"The school dance. I have to go for the newspaper."

Mom shook her head. "They cannot force you. So you do not have to go."

Funny, that's exactly the point I tried to make to Isabel. But coming from my mother, all of a sudden I felt the urge to disagree.

"I have to go."

She pursed her lips and wouldn't make eye contact with me — the highest form of dismissal. "No, you can't. I won't allow it."

With those words, a familiar rage reared its ugly head. Hearing my mother say "I won't allow it" gave me flashbacks to all the things I wasn't allowed to do growing up: attend sleepovers, experiment with nail polish, ride the bus, dye my hair, wear heels (well, I wouldn't do that anyway — but it's the principle!).

"Why not?" I whined.

My mom looked around and hissed out of the corner of her mouth, "Keep your voice down! You're not going to a dance. It's unnecessary, and it's only something that poorly raised American kids do. You should be concentrating on your schoolwork, not stuff like that. Nonsense like that is why American students are behind the rest of the world in academics."

"Mom, I hate to break it to you, but I'M one of those 'American students.' As much as you hate to admit it, I am NOT Korean."

My mom stopped in her tracks and gave me her Death Stare. The stare that made my soul shrivel up into a scared little worm. A shriveled-up worm that pooped its pants.

"You think you're American?" she asked in an eerily calm voice.

I looked down at my feet and muttered, "Yes."

Her icy words stabbed into the top of my head. "Well, then. I guess I am not your mother."

All I could do was follow her meekly back to the car. A part of me was angry at her for being so ridiculously strict, and the other part of me felt guilty for some reason. I was American, you know? Well, Korean American anyway. Why couldn't my mom just accept that?

When we got home, my mom gave me the silent treatment, so I hid out in my room. I plopped down onto my bed and sighed, and decided to seek solace in my hidden DVD stash.

I crawled under the bed and took out a box filled with DVDs I'd collected over the years. Movies like *The Notebook*, *Pretty in Pink*, *27 Dresses*, *How to Lose a Guy in 10 Days*, *Chocolat*, and *Roman Holiday*.

Yes, it's true.

I AM OBSESSED WITH ROMANTIC MOVIES.

Oh, the shame. I've had to keep it a secret because if Carrie and David ever found out, I'd be ridiculed to death. I shivered just thinking about it.

I took out *Pretty in Pink* and popped it into my laptop. The plot of this movie is ludicrous — Molly Ringwald's "alternative" character (the '80s equivalent of an American Apparel–sporting hipster girl) falls for this rich guy from "the other side of town" (the '80s equivalent of a douche bag. Or did the '80s invent douche bags?). They face adversity, yada yada, and wind up, in the end, kissing at the dance.

Even this outcast girl with her sad-sap dad was allowed to go to the dance. Albeit in the most hideous handmade pink dress ever.

I felt like I lived in a totally different world from Molly Ringwald's character. And from everyone else in reality.

The simplest things for most of the people I knew, like going to a school dance, were always such a torturous trial with my parents. Why couldn't I just say, "Hi, Mom and Dad, guess what? I get to go to the Homecoming dance!" And then my alternate-reality mom would clasp her hands together and say, "Oh, my little girl is growing up! We'll have to get you a beautiful new dress!" and wipe a tear from her eye. Then my alternate-reality dad would beam proudly and say, "Who's the lucky boy who gets to take you to this shindig?" with a pipe in hand.

Okay, well, apparently my alternate-reality parents also lived in the 1950s.

My Korean-reality parents: Mom freaks out and thinks only devil children go to dances. Because she's secretly afraid I might get pregnant dancing with a boy. I wonder if my mother really knows how babies are made? Dad is totally disinterested, doesn't really understand what a "dance" is, and when he finds out I have to purchase things to attend will be adamantly against it. This is the man who made me use sticky rice as glue for art projects because he found Elmer's glue to be an unnecessary extravagance.

There was no way around it. My mother could not be reasoned with, and my dad would definitely not take my side on this one.

I'd have to sneak my way to the Homecoming dance.

I called up David.

"What up, Hizzle."

"Hey. So um, you have to help me."

"Do I have to?"

I resisted the urge to stick my arm into the phone to punch his face on the other line. "YES, butt-wipe."

"Well, since you're asking so nicely . . ."

"I have to figure out a way to go to the Homecoming dance without my parents knowing."

I swear I heard David choke on something.

"David? David! Come on, get with the program!"

He sputtered, "Get with the program? What are you, some '80s PE coach?"

"No! Now help me get to the dance!"

"Okay, the first, most like, glaring question being: WHY are you going to the dance? Did someone ask you?" he asked incredulously.

I stared at the phone for a few seconds, contemplating hanging up on him.

"Hellooo, Holly?"

"Mm hm. I'm just wondering, why are we friends again?"

"Because I am a handsome addition to your group of otherwise hideous friends."

I sighed. "I'm going to the dance because *The Weasel Times* is sending me to cover it, like it's some huge event that affects the world, or something."

"Are you serious?"

"Yeah, hello. Why the hell else would I go to this thing?"

"So you *don't* have a date?"

"Ew, no. But anyway, how am I going to get a dress, get ready for the dance undercover, and stay out that late without my mom calling the SWAT team to come after me?"

"Hm. That's a tough one. Well, the dress is easy. Doesn't Liz have a billion of those things?"

"Um, yeah, but Liz and I aren't exactly the same size. She has these things called boobs that make it difficult for me to fit into her stuff."

A sound of disgust came from David's end. "Okay, if you want to keep this conversation going you need to not bring up Liz's boobs."

By the end of the phone call we had devised a plan. Both David and I had some money saved from New Year's (we may get screwed in other ways, but on New Year's Asian kids make bank), and he kindly offered to pool some money to help buy a dress. In return, I told him he could come as my date. As long as he knew it wasn't a date.

"Wow, thanks. So romantic. Just like I've always dreamed," he said sarcastically.

"So do you have to lie to your parents?" I asked hopefully.

I could almost see David's shrug over the phone. "Nah. They don't care."

"That's so unfair," I protested. "Why aren't your parents as uptight as mine?"

"Um, because my dad is second-generation Chinese, not crazy Korean. And because I am a boy, and therefore worthier of responsibilities and privileges."

"Oh, right. I forgot about the whole boy thing. As a girl

I must be a good little student and do my math homework at my parents' side every night of the week. Otherwise, other Korean people will think I am a ho."

We both started cracking up. I couldn't be a ho even if I was decked out in fishnets on Hollywood Boulevard. People would probably just offer me a ride home to my mommy.

"Okay, okay, so on Homecoming night I'll be 'working on a journalism deadline at school.' My parents can only call me on my cell phone, then."

"But don't your parents know when the dance is? Isn't this all highly suspicious?"

I snorted. "Please. They don't know the date of the dance. Who do you think I am? I was twenty steps ahead of them from step one."

"Okay, whatever that means."

My plans were set. I would buy a dress, hide it at Liz's, pretend to ride my bike to school, get ready at Liz's, then go to the dance, and arrive at home by 11:00 P.M. wearing my jeans again.

This would be the most rebellious thing that Holly Kim had ever done. Yes, lying to my parents was the most awful thing I could do. Lying to my mother was . . . I shuddered. Inconceivable.

Just then my mom popped her head into my room. "Are you still SULKING?" she asked.

Always the peacemaker. "I'm not sulking," I replied moodily.

"*Don't* give me that look. Anyway, it's time for dinner, so get up and try to be helpful," she barked before leaving.

She left the door wide open, knowing full well how much that infuriated me.

I glared at her retreating back. Then I grabbed my cell phone to make one last call.

"Hey, Liz? So do you *finally* want to take me shopping?"

The wheels were in motion.

SIX

. . . .

PETTY MUDSLINGING BEGINS AS
HOMECOMING WEEK APPROACHES

These buttons are fugly."

I hit David in the arm. "Shh! Carrie designed them."

"So? It doesn't mean they're not fug."

I resisted the urge to giggle. It was true, the buttons Carrie made for Liz's Homecoming campaign were hideous: brown with huge bubbly, orange letters that spelled out LIZ IZ QUEEN. But she had a button-making machine at home (one of many weird contraptions Carrie had in her arsenal of crafty things) and we were trying to be supportive.

We brought the buttons because the Homecoming Court nominations were being announced at lunch. I thought Carrie had been premature by making them because we didn't know if Liz would be nominated, but she insisted that she would be. I looked at them in their brown-and-orange glory and bit my tongue.

Spotting Liz and Carrie across the Quad, I waved them over. David quickly hid the buttons in his backpack.

"Are you nervous?" I asked Liz. She was wringing her hands; and her hair, which was usually perfect, looked a little disheveled.

"No! Yes. I mean, kinda!" she said hysterically. Whoa, this flustered state was very un-Liz-like.

Carrie patted her arm. "Don't worry, Liz. You got this in the bag!"

David and I exchanged looks that said otherwise.

A crackle on the PA system shut everyone up.

"Yo, yo, yo, BHS, it's that moment you've all been waiting for! The Homecoming Court announcements! Who's going to be BHS royalty this fall?"

I refrained from gagging. Our student body president, Martin Wong, ran through the male nominees first — every single one of the guys was a jock. Typical.

"Yeah, yeah, Matthew Reynolds and company, blah blah," Carrie said. "Let's move on!"

"And now for the lovely ladies of the BHS Homecoming Court!" An obnoxious chuckle came through the speakers. Martin was such a dork.

Liz clasped my hands and then Carrie's. I smiled nervously at her. "Our Homecoming Court princesses and potential queen are, in alphabetical order . . . Jessamin Aya!" One corner of the Quad erupted in noise. I craned my neck to see the hipsters hugging Jessamin, who tried to look bored.

"Lola Chang!" The Asian Christian group cheered, the girls giggling and jumping around Lola.

"Candace Ferrera!" A huge roar went up in the middle of the Quad where Candace and the Barbies were hanging out. I glanced at Carrie and David, who were looking as anxious as I felt.

"Lauren Muklashy!" Candace's group cheered again, though not as loudly. Lauren was merely second fiddle to Candace.

There was only one spot left on the Homecoming Court. I got ready to console Liz. I really hoped she wouldn't take it too hard — I still found this entire thing so dumb.

"And last, but definitely not least . . . Elizabeth Rezapour!"

Carrie whooped, jumping up and down and hugging Liz, whose eyes were wide with disbelief. David stood there with his mouth open, and I smiled widely before noticing Candace's group openly glaring at us, their heavily lined eyes boring holes into Liz's head.

I tried to ignore the creepy Barbie dolls. "Liz, you did it!" It actually happened!

She unleashed her megawatt grin. "I can't believe it!"

David opened his backpack with a flourish. "Well, believe it, dude! We're already prepared!"

Liz picked one of the buttons up and started laughing once she read it. "Nice! No time like the present to start my Homecoming Queen campaign, right?"

We walked over to our lunch spot and Liz immediately pulled out a notebook and started scribbling in it. I sat down next to her, trying to see what she was writing.

"Holls, did you seriously make all your journalism staff nominate Liz?" Carrie asked before taking a bite of her hummus-and-veggie sandwich.

I looked away from Liz's notebook. "Sure. They're the biggest group of anti-school-spirit people so they were happy to nominate someone who's not on student government."

"And I got the Mathletes in on that," David bragged, adjusting his knit beanie over his messy hair.

"Did you promise all of them a date with Liz?" Carrie asked.

Liz snorted while furiously writing in her notebook. "Please."

"Uh, can we go back to the Mathletes? I can't believe you joined this year," I teased.

David reached over lightning quick and pulled my sweatshirt hood over my head. "What about it, Miss Remedial Algebra?"

"*Pardonnez moi*, I'm in geometry this year, thank you very much."

"Yeah! With ME!" Carrie announced proudly. We both wriggled our eyebrows exaggeratedly at each other. David rolled his eyes and started eating his lunch.

I noticed Liz had finished writing. "What is that?" I asked, peering at the notebook. She handed it over.

HOMECOMING COURT HIT LIST

1. *Candace Ferrera — Witch. Was the ringleader in starting a rumor about my boobs. Also, once threw a plate of sloppy joes into Carrie's face in fourth grade. Sociopathic cow. THE one to beat.*

2. *Lauren Muklashy — Brainless follower of Candace, probably was "allowed" to be nominated just to be witch's handmaid. Once called Holly a "geisha."*

3. *Lola Chang — Horrible human being. Stole Ryan Patel from shy albino girl, Melanie Duger, for Halloween dance in eighth grade.*

4. *Jessamin Aya — Aside from her ridiculous name, she once kicked David's skateboard on purpose and giggled while walking away with friends. Can't tell if it was a ploy for his attentions or pure witchery. Annoying hipster either way.*

I was shocked but also felt kind of vindicated — this Homecoming Queen insanity was all for revenge!

"Dude, LIZ!" I exclaimed.

She lifted her chin defiantly. "What?"

"Don't 'what' me! Is this why you're running for Homecoming Queen?"

David and Carrie both looked at Liz's notebook curiously. Carrie asked, "What are you guys talking about?"

I pointed at the list. "She has like, a creepy hit list for the Homecoming Court. All the girls' names plus a description of her beef with them. Liz, you're like the comic book vigilante of school dances."

"I want to see!" David lunged for the notebook.

"Me too!" Carrie crowed.

Liz handed it to them. "Fine, whatever. It's no secret I hate all these hags."

I shook my head. "Yeah but, Liz, this is a whole lot of trouble, don't you think? Just for some, what, popularity revenge? I didn't think you cared about that."

"It's not revenge per se. I just want to make a point."

Carrie looked up from the list. "Which is?"

"That I'm better than them."

David let out a whistle. "Okay, then."

Hands on her skinny-jeans-clad hips, she said, "What? It's true, isn't it? EVERYONE'S better than them. They suck as human beings and they need to be brought down a notch or two."

"I mean, yeah, of course they all suck. But why bother? It's been a long time since you've cared about what those girls thought," I said.

"Yes, it's been too long. I know how much these jerks care about something as trivial as this. I want to crush their dreams."

"Yes!" Carrie cried, laughing.

David and I looked at each other. This was just plain weird and out of Liz's too-cool-for-school character.

"What? Don't look at each other in your little secret way. I'm not doing anything wrong," Liz said angrily.

I sighed. "I don't think it's wrong. . . . Just a bit . . . pointless."

David stared at the buttons. "Yeah. I thought this was just like, really important to you. I felt bad we made fun of you, even. And I never feel bad about making fun of you."

Tears welled up in Liz's perfectly mascaraed eyes. "FINE! Don't help me, then!" With that, she snatched the buttons from him and stormed off.

The three of us were left, once again, looking helplessly at each other.

"Wow," I said, for lack of anything better to say.

"I think you guys need to get off your high horses and just let Liz do what she wants," Carrie huffed.

"What high horse?! I'm all for revenge, if it works! But I mean . . . is she really going to be satisfied when she wins Homecoming Queen? Is this a satisfying type of revenge? Why not just trip them in public?" I asked.

David crossed his arms. "Yeah, it's not going to do anything. Maybe for like five minutes. She's been holding this crap in foreeever."

"Yes, she has. So shouldn't we just keep our mouths shut and let her do what she wants?" Carrie asked.

"I never keep my mouth shut," I said.

*   *   *

When I walked into journalism later that day, Isabel was having a complete meltdown. I approached her slumped body apprehensively. "Um, are you okay?"

With her face plastered onto a printout of the Homecoming Court spread, her muffled voice replied, "Thith footpid sfred int gong tbe ruddy ontyme."

"What?"

When her head sprang up her eyes were teary. She pushed her curly black hair out of her face. "I said this stupid spread isn't going to be ready on time. The printers are backed up this month so we need to send the November issue to print earlier than planned — which means we won't have our King and Queen profiles in time!"

Sometimes kids take things so seriously. I looked down at the unfinished spread when I felt Isabel's eyes boring into my head. "Hey. HOLLY."

"Uh, yes?"

"Isn't Mrs. Richards your English teacher?"

Confused, I answered, "Yeah."

"She's one of the ballot counters."

"Yeah?" I asked, still confused.

"Must I spell it out, Holly?" Isabel asked impatiently. "Ask her who's going to win."

"Huh? How would she know?!"

Isabel gave me a pitying look. "Oh, Holly, do you really think we actually *vote* on the King and Queen?"

"Um, yes? Do we not live in the United States of *America*?"

"No, we go to *high school*. And here, the most popular student government member always wins Homecoming

66

Court. Which is probably going to be Candace Ferrera or Lauren what's-her-name. And we need to find out who it is so we can get this issue done in time."

I couldn't care less about our deadline at this point. "Are you saying the election is *fixed?*"

Isabel nodded her head slowly.

"How do you even know this?!"

She shrugged. "It's info that's passed down from one generation of newspaper staff to the next. One of the student government's many dirty little secrets."

"Has anyone ever bothered finding out if it's *true* and exposing it?" I asked incredulously.

"Oh, Holly. Still so optimistic about the power of the press. It's just a dumb high school thing. We have other things to worry about."

"Like *what?* Who's going to be our next assistant girls' softball coach?" I was livid. "So you want me to call Mrs. Richards? Sure, I'll call her."

Isabel followed me as I stomped toward the classroom phone. "All right, but be subtle, okay? There's a tactful way to do all of this. . . ."

"Oh, sure thing!" I said with false cheerfulness. Isabel stood by me fretfully.

Thus, the birth of my treachery. Moments later I was asking Mrs. Richards if she could help out the paper by disclosing the names of the Homecoming Queen and King ahead of time because we were behind on our deadline.

"But, Holly, how would I know this information? The elections are next week!"

My voice took on a conspiratorial tone. "Oh, it's okay, Mrs. Richards, I know all about the rigging. Is it Candace?"

Isabel's eyes got huge. "You can't actually SAY it!" she hissed. When I shook my head at her, she shoved her ear next to the phone so that she could listen in. I tried pushing her away, but I have stick arms and Isabel is the captain of the varsity volleyball team.

There was a pause on the other line. "Does Mr. Green know you're asking me this?"

Mr. Green was the student government advisor. "Yeah, sure!" I said with what I hoped was confidence.

Some more silence. "I don't know, Holly, I'm sorry. I don't feel comfortable having this conversation. Good-bye, now."

Damn. I was hoping she would actually admit to something.

Isabel smacked my shoulder when I hung up the phone. "HOLLY! *What* did you just do?"

My bravado left me as suddenly as it came. Did I just make a huge mistake? "I was going to get her to admit the thing was rigged," I said.

"ARE YOU NUTS?! I told you to be subtle! We can't actually say it *outright*!" she screeched. "You better hope this doesn't get to Mr. Green."

She walked away and I was left feeling more scared than angry.

When school was over that day, I still couldn't shake the feeling. I sat on the front lawn, waiting for Carrie so we could walk home together.

I spotted her, with Liz. Carrie made a face at me that clearly said, "*Be nice.*"

"Hey," I greeted them apprehensively.

Liz gave me a shy smile. "Hey. Sorry about earlier."

Relief washed over me. Fighting with friends was up there on my Hate List, right above wearing headgear for three years.

"I'm sorry, too. And I didn't mean to be so unsupportive of your revenge plan," I said in a rush.

"Is it revenge? I guess I *am* being a little crazy."

I was dying to tell her about what I learned in journalism that day when Candace Ferrera and her gang of identical lemmings walked by.

Candace stopped in front of Liz. "Wow, so, good job today. Did you have to pay people to nominate you?" The girls behind her burst into giggles, some gleefully covering their mouths. I wanted to punch them.

Liz whipped out her most condescending smile. "Great theory, Einstein. Whatever helps you sleep at night." This time Carrie and I giggled hysterically, covering our mouths mockingly.

Candace whipped her head around and focused her evil eye on us. "Oh, shut *up*, dorks." I flinched. It was *not* cool being the underdog in a high school movie. I felt Carrie move forward and I grabbed her before she did something stupid.

"Say that *again!*" she shot out. Oh, how I wished at that moment that I had the perfect comeback. But my tongue was tied. My sassy mouth when I wrote my column was one thing — real-life Holly was still wimpier than I wanted to admit.

Candace sent Carrie a withering look, then returned her attentions to Liz. "I'll *never* understand why you decided to hang out with these losers. Honestly, it's only sophomore year. It's not too late to come back to us. You know you're actually one of us, right?"

My mouth dropped open. Was this bitch *serious*? Did she think we were acting out a scene from *Mean Girls*? Where were Lindsay Lohan and Rachel McAdams? No, seriously, where were they?

"I have *nothing* in common with you. Don't *ever* think you can talk to me or my friends like this again. I'm being nice. You better *appreciate*," Liz said with an icy calm that freaked even me out. I wondered if those rumors about her uncle being in the Persian mafia were true after all.

Candace looked startled, then regained her composure. "What*ever*. I guess it feels nice to be the big fish in such a crappy pond." With that, she and her lemmings walked away.

Carrie glowered, her hands balled into fists. "I *hate* them."

Liz, in contrast, held up shaky hands. "Wow. I can't believe she finally had the nerve to confront me."

I decided at that moment to not tell Liz about the election rigging. I wanted her to have her revenge, rigged or not.

SEVEN

. . . .

HIGH SCHOOL RIVALRY DATES BACK TO A TIME WHEN THERE WAS NO INTERNET

Please shoot me the day I wear anything like this."

Liz glanced over at the poofy pink princess gown I was holding and shrugged. "It's not that bad." Carrie met my eyes and pretended to gag.

I shook my head sadly. "Oh, Liz, it's already too late for you."

She narrowed her eyes at me and shoved a couple dresses into my arms. "Oh, shut up and try these on already."

I was out shopping for my Homecoming dress that weekend with Carrie and Liz, and so far we had been to what seemed like a billion stores without any success. I could feel Carrie growing listless, but Liz promised this would be the last one. I hoped so. I was starting to get depressed.

In the fitting room, I looked with skepticism at the two dresses Liz had picked out. One was a short, sleeveless teal dress with a skinny belt looped around it. Cute, but everything looked cute before I wore it on my boobless frame. The other was a flowy, long, pale blue dress with a cool racer back and layers of fabric overlapping on the skirt part. Really pretty but, again . . . ?

I pulled on the blue one first. It hung straight to the floor and made my skinny shoulders look like a hanger. "Ugh!"

Liz tapped the door. "Don't 'ugh' yet! Let me see!"

I opened the door and made a face. She looked me up and down. "Not bad. You look like a young Kate Moss."

"Ha! Nice try. That's another way of saying I look emaciated and awkward."

Liz didn't argue. "Well, the color looks great on you, and it's such a cool style. A lot of girls would kill to look as . . . willowy as you."

I made a face. "Olive Oyl is not the look I'm going for. Next!"

The next dress fit me more snugly, and I had to say, with the little flare of the skirt, it was fun to twirl around in. When I opened the door Liz's eyes lit up. "Oh, this is PERFECT."

Carrie ran over. "Let me see!" She whistled appreciatively. "You look great! Like a right proper lady!" she said in a British accent.

I suddenly felt shy. "Really? It doesn't look too girly?"

Liz threw up her hands in exasperation. "Holly! Sometimes 'girly' is *not* a dirty word. You look *amazing* in this!"

I eyed myself in the mirror again. The belt did help give the illusion of a figure. Now if only my legs could miraculously grow calf muscles.

I paid for the dress and we headed home in Liz's car. "Wow, we're actually going to a school dance," Carrie mused from the backseat.

"Thanks for agreeing to be my date, Carrie," Liz said from behind the wheel.

"No prob, dude. I'll just go to prom with Scott," she responded cheerfully.

"Keep dreaming!" I said.

Carrie kicked my seat from behind. "Dreams come true, you know. Hey, so how's the covert mission going with your parents?"

"So far so good. They know I'll be 'working' all weekend, and they didn't bat an eye when I told them," I said with satisfaction.

"Your parents are so trusting," Liz said. "Mine interrogate me about *everything*. They're always worried that I'll become a prostitute at any moment." It was true, Liz's parents threw the word "prostitute" around about as often as my parents used the phrase "bad daughter."

"They're only letting me go to the dance because I'm nominated for Homecoming Queen," she continued. "They think it's a weird American tradition, but my mother loves any opportunity to take me to the spa."

"Spa?!" Carrie sputtered. "I'm sorry, are you preparing for your royal wedding night? I thought you were just going to the Homecoming dance."

"Persian women know how to take care of themselves, thank you very much."

I was envious. "I wish my mom would let me wear makeup, let alone take me to get primped and preened."

"Uh, guys? Must I remind you that my mom is *making* my dress? With her own hands? Enough said," Carrie said with finality.

"I guess everyone's parents are crazy," I said. "But mine are still the worst."

When Liz dropped me off I left the dress with her. She placed her hand solemnly over her heart and said, "I shall guard it with my life."

I looked at it a little wistfully before she drove off. It was so ridiculous that I couldn't keep my dress in my own house. But my mom was no stranger to rifling through my closet searching for something or another, so it was a sacrifice I had to make.

Sitting in bio the next day, I was completely ignoring the lesson that I, of course, didn't really understand nor care to understand. (Mitosis? What? Good God, what is all this ABOUT? Do people really understand science? I suspect that all scientists pretend to understand what the heck they're talking about because they're too scared to look stupid in front of all the other scientists. Yes, that must be it.)

When the class was interrupted by someone stepping in and handing Mrs. Robinson a note, I felt a nervous sense of déjà vu. And wouldn't you know, seconds after she read the note, Mrs. Robinson looked straight at me. Before she could say anything, I got up with a sigh and grabbed my things. I walked up to her with a weary, "Where should I go?"

She handed me the pass and said in a low voice, "The principal's office."

As if I didn't already have a (wholly undeserved) messed-up reputation! The class broke into whispers and murmurs. Even I was a little shocked. What in God's name could I have done to get called to the Mother of All Offices?

I fled the classroom as fast as I could. As I walked across the empty Quad, I grew more nervous. Could this be about me talking to Mrs. Richards? No way . . . I mean, what's the big deal? I didn't think Mrs. Richards would have told on me to the principal. I racked my brain for other nefarious activities I may have been involved in without knowing it.

By the time I reached the office, I was sweating with all the minor evil deeds I had done recently. Never had I felt more wicked. I absentmindedly carved my name into my math class desk once. But who the heck hasn't? Also, I've hid under the bleachers on more than one PE occasion. Oh, God, I'm dead. I approached Principal Mendel's office with a knot in my stomach. The principal's secretary nodded me in.

The instant I saw who else was in the office, I knew why I was called in there. Sitting at his desk was Principal Mendel, and standing in opposite corners of the room were Mr. Williams and the student government advisor, Mr. Green.

"Holly. Sit down." Principal Mendel pointed at a chair sternly. Principal Mendel is one of those men that you know are supposed to scare you, but they never quite do it. He has the mustache and everything. But David recently pointed to why his authoritativeness fails: "He's really, really not smart."

However, I admit it. I was terrified.

I sat down. Before anyone could open their mouth, someone else came through the door behind me. I turned my head.

"LIZ?"

Liz walked in, looking equally confused. "Holly?"

I was now completely thrown off guard. "What's all this about?" I asked.

At that, Mr. Green marched over to me, stopped two inches away from my face, and spat out, "Nice try, Holly. I spoke to Mrs. Richards and she told me all about your little ploy."

I'm not too embarrassed to say that tears started pricking my eyes. I mean, I was being chastised by a huge man who looked like a celebrity bodyguard. Who drove a Mazda Miata but was still scary. I felt the dread in my stomach growing, creeping its way throughout my entire body.

"Ploy? I didn't do anything wrong," I said in a small shaky voice, without as much conviction as I'd hoped. Oh, Lord. Was I going to get suspended? Would I be able to go to college? Would my mom beat me with a rolled-up newspaper like that time I came home late from the movies? I truly felt scared, and at that moment regretted being born.

But it was so unfair. *They* were the ones rigging the election! Weren't they?

Mr. Green sat down but kept talking. "*The Weasel Times*

is always pulling this underhanded crap. You have to follow the rules like everyone else."

"I wasn't trying to pull anything!" I sputtered. "I just . . . we needed to know who the Queen and King were for our deadline."

Mr. Green gave a short bark of a laugh and I jumped a little in my seat. "How could anyone know that when no one has voted yet? You basically implied to Mrs. Richards that it was rigged."

Liz's head whipped toward me with a questioning look.

I was surrounded by adults who were in charge, and I had no power in this situation. I felt like there was nothing I could say to make this go any other way than they had already decided it would go. This was so WRONG. I tried to summon up some courage. "Well, that's the rumor."

Mr. Green's face turned dangerously red. "A rumor started by *The Weasel Times*, no doubt!"

Mr. Williams finally spoke up. "Oh come off it, Jeff. We all know it's true."

Liz finally reacted. "Wait, WHAT?"

Principal Mendel stood up in a huff. "Settle down, Mr. Williams. This is not the time to be making unfounded accusations. Anyway, we brought Miss Rezapour here for a reason. Miss Kim, we know you did this because your little friend here was nominated for Homecoming Queen."

"What does that have to do with anything?" Liz asked frostily. It was very queenlike, actually.

Mr. Green raised his eyebrow and dismissively replied, "We know you put her up to this."

"EXCUSE me?!" Liz said incredulously, raising her voice.

I, on the other hand, am usually very polite to authority figures. Almost to a fault. I blame it on my Korean upbringing, which upholds the idea that one needs to show utmost respect to anyone who is even one month older (and therefore wiser) than you. To act any other way would be an embarrassment to your parents and your country.

But at that moment, authority figures be damned, I was pissed. Liz and I were being majorly and unfairly dissed.

"She did NOT put me up to this! She didn't even know until this moment that the election might be fixed. I decided to find out if it was," I said angrily.

"You wanted to sway Mrs. Richards's decision. You thought she would treat you specially because you're her student," Mr. Green said accusingly.

I tried to remain calm. "You are twisting my words. Why would I even think that? Mrs. Richards wasn't really making a decision, was she? She's just supposed to count votes like you say!"

Principal Mendel and Mr. Green both exchanged strange glances. Crossing his arms over his chest, Mr. Williams asked, "Well, isn't she?"

Principal Mendel waved his hand dismissively. "Whatever the case, what Holly did was highly unethical, accusing the student government of such things based on nothing but speculation. And to use her position at the paper to try and sway the decision in favor of her friend."

"But . . . I DIDN'T!" I said in a super loud voice that startled even me.

"I know you have to lie to cover this up, Holly, but it's really not a good idea," Mr. Green said. The condescension in his voice triggered daydreams of dropkicking his shaved head across the room.

Principal Mendel sighed. "Well, it looks like it's your word against ours. Therefore, as punishment, Miss Rezapour, you are disqualified from the competition and will step down from the Homecoming Court. As for you, Miss Kim, consider yourself lucky that all I'm going to do is ban you from the dance. *The Weasel Times* will not get to cover the Homecoming dance this year."

I was shocked. I looked over at Liz, who was strangely stone-faced.

Once we were in the hallway I looked at Liz apprehensively. "Sorry about that, Liz. I had no idea this would happen. I should have told you about the whole election thing."

She took a deep breath. "You don't have to be sorry. I can't believe they can just get away with accusing us of stuff we didn't do!"

"I know! I mean, yes, I did maybe overstep my boundaries. But, I still think the election is rigged! Mr. Williams said as much."

Just then Mr. Williams walked out of the office and patted my back. "Tough break, Holly. But sometimes it's easier to humor these guys."

GREAT ADVICE. More inspiration from the people that were supposedly grown-ups. If being a grown-up meant being a compromising chump, then no thanks.

Liz shrugged her shoulders. "Oh well."

I felt really bad. "Are you sure you don't mind? I'm so sorry, Liz. I know you wanted to be Homecoming Queen."

"Maybe I did. But honestly, it's not worth all this trouble. I'm kind of sick of it already."

"Are you sure? Maybe I can still —"

"Dude. For reals, no worries. I'm sorry you can't go to the dance either. That dress!"

Hm. Strange, I had forgotten until that moment that I was being punished, too. I should have been relieved.

Right?

"Rewind that! Please rewind that!"

The DVD player blipped and showed Sissy Spacek getting drenched by pig's blood again.

Carrie, David, and I squealed with glee and horror. Liz groaned and shoved her head farther into a pillow.

"You guys can be so sick sometimes," Liz said once it was safe to open her eyes again. "I mean, what kind of freaks sit at home and watch *Carrie* the night of the Homecoming dance?"

"Us," David said through a mouthful of Doritos that he had snuck into Carrie's basement. "But the more pressing question is, what kind of freak sits with her freak friends watching *Carrie* on Homecoming night in a Homecoming *gown*?"

Patting her silky chiffon skirt, Liz happily replied, "Homecoming Queen Elizabeth."

"You lucked out, huh, Holly?" Carrie asked while shoving some chips into her mouth. Even Carrie caved to junk food when we watched movies.

I smiled. "Yup, lucked out." The thing was, I had actually been looking forward to the dance. It would have been fun to go with my friends, to get to wear a dress that didn't look ugly on me for once. But I wasn't ready to admit that yet. Instead I looked at Liz regretfully. "Sorry, again, to take you down with me. There goes your revenge."

She shrugged. "You were right. It was a lot of work for something that wasn't worth it in the end. Would have been great, though," she said with an exaggerated wink. I was also wearing my dress. Over jeans.

"I think the fury of Holly's mom could have been *amazing* if she was caught," David said.

Carrie groaned. "IF she was caught. But seriously, Holls, your mom needs to chill!"

Liz looked at me sympathetically. "If it makes you feel better, my dad said he would have sent one of my male cousins as a chaperone if I went with a date. That's why I wanted to take Carrie."

Carrie let out a peal of laughter. "What? Both of your parents are nuts."

"Sorry, not all our parents can be hippies that encourage talking about your feelings and boundaries all the time!"

Carrie sighed dramatically. "That can get annoying, too, you know."

"You'll never understand our pain," David said while kicking his feet up on the coffee table.

"Oh, please, David. Your parents are more American than mine," Carrie retorted defensively. "Except that your dad wants you to be a doctor with an almost psychotic drive."

"You can take the boy out of China, but you can't take China out of the boy," David said with a shrug.

"Well, just because my parents aren't old-fashionedy immigrants doesn't mean my life is all easy," said Carrie.

"No one said it was. But at least you're allowed to wear nail polish." I pointed to her hands.

Carrie looked at her neon-green nails and nodded. "That's true. But at least you can buy new jeans."

I looked down at my crisp jeans and sighed happily. Carrie's parents had strong feelings about fair labor and living sustainably — all her clothes were either thrifted, made by her mom (hence, her Homecoming dress that never was), or made by some eco-designer from Etsy.com. Luckily, Carrie could pull it off. If it were me, I would have looked like some seriously misguided hobo off the streets.

Liz shrugged her shoulders and patted down her four-hundred-dollar dress. "Nobody has the perfect family."

And at those words, we heard Carrie's mom yell from upstairs, "Do you kids want some whole-grain acai berry muffins? I can also make kale smoothies."

David almost choked on his M&M'S as Carrie yelled out, "MOOOM!"

LETTERS TO THE EDITOR

Looks like the student government proved you wrong. The dance was a huge success and the decorations were beautiful. IN YOUR FACE.
— THE COLLECTIVE MEMBERS OF THE
BHS STUDENT GOVERNMENT

The dance sucked. It was in the gym. No amount of Christmas lights and cardboard fountains could hide the bleachers and rubber floor. The entire student government needs to be impeached for stupidity.
— ANONYMOUS, JUNIOR

Holly's column was rude as usual. She owes the Homecoming Court an apology. She almost ruined it for us! And she was obviously trying to rig the thing for Elizabeth Rezapour. No one believes your fake-ass excuses, Holly!
— CANDACE F., SOPHOMORE

If anyone says Holly tried to rig the election, kindly tell them to SHUT UP. And take off those ugly knockoff boots already, Candace. We all know they ain't Prada.
— ELIZABETH R., SOPHOMORE

NOVEMBER

A long, long time ago a bunch of English people were made fun of a lot in their own country because they wore giant buckles on their hats and ruffled blouses. Oh, yes, and they were also uptight religious puritans who got on everyone's nerves.

So, because they couldn't handle the teasing — or I suppose they called it "religious persecution" — they came over on three big boats to the United States of America. Except back then they called it the New World, or Big Island o' Savages.

They came over and were like, "Oh, oops, perhaps we should have brushed up on our *Complete Idiot's Guide to Settling in Different Continents*." Because they didn't know that it got really, really cold in Massachusetts. And that the soil there wasn't exactly the same as the Motherland's and therefore they couldn't plant all those infernal cabbages.

And also, they were freaked out by the Native Americans. (Back then, they called them "savages," and then for the next two hundred years Americans called them "Indians," which was just willful ignorance since we knew full well at this point that no one had landed in India.)

So there these settlers were, starving, diseased, and scared for the upcoming winter. Which would consequently kick their ass in coldness and length. (Did you know that on the East Coast winter lasts until like, June? JUNE! WTF! San Diego, I kiss your sandy shores.)

Lo and behold, the scary, scary Native American people took pity on these skinny intruders and offered them food from their harvest. I don't know if a cornucopia was actually involved in any of this, but I imagine a chief of some tribe carried over a cornucopia full of corn and turkeys and handed it over to them.

They called this sharing of foods and good times Thanksgiving.

I could go into a lot of things — like how the Pilgrims that we all know and love weren't technically the first group of folks to have a Thanksgiving in America. (I think people hung out in Florida and Virginia first, but they never get any love.) Or how I think the Native Americans were badass for sharing their food when they could have easily watched the people who invaded their turf and gave them smallpox starve to death. (DO NOT GOOGLE "SMALLPOX"

UNLESS YOU WANT YOUR EYEBALLS BURNED
OUT OF YOUR SKULL.)

Anyway. I hope you all remember to give thanks this year. Even if you are forced to have dinner with fifty of your closest relatives in small quarters, with screaming children's sticky gravy fingers grabbing at you, with uncles belching in front of the TV, and with aunts making comments about your acne. If my family survives this dinner alive, we should all be thankful.

Gobble Gobble,

Holly

EIGHT

. . . .

**TEEN TRIES TO ESCAPE ANNOYING
FAMILY YEAR AFTER YEAR; FAILS**

Why were you in the shower for so long?"

"Are you SERIOUSLY asking me this, Mom?"

"Yes! I am very serious, Holly."

"Why?! Are you monitoring my showers or something, you psycho?"

"Wha?! Monitoring?! Now your mother can't even ask you a simple question without being crazy?"

I was standing in the hallway with a towel wrapped around my head, ready to smash it into the wall repeatedly. A girl couldn't even take a shower in the Kim house without being interrogated about it afterward.

"Mom, you are insane. Good-bye." I stalked off to my room and slammed the door. (But only kinda — if I really slammed the door it would be busted down in a Mom-shaped tornado, and I was in no mood for a natural disaster.)

I flopped onto my bed and screamed into my pillow. Good God, my family was driving me crazy. It was just the usual Saturday:

7:00 A.M. Woke up to my mom rummaging through my drawers looking for some socks she thought she might have put in my laundry by mistake. I'm not allowed to have locks on my door. Tried to fall back asleep through anger.

9:00 A.M. Sat down to breakfast with my family and was greeted with the usual "Ohhh, look who finally decided to join us!" It's 9:00 A.M. Let's calm down.

10:00 A.M. Fought with my sister over doing the dishes. Ann appears to think she actually does them once in a while. She's completely deluded. I ended the fight by soaking her shirt with soapsuds and took gleeful yet slightly guilty pleasure in her stomping to her room to change.

10:30 A.M. Forced into accompanying my dad to the fish market. He made me hold the fish as he dawdled around the store for an infinite amount of time. We were buying some extra seafood for the Thanksgiving feast that was going to be held at our house the following week. Yes, FISH. My dad always has to spice things up Korean-style at these holiday gatherings.

12:00 P.M. Came home to my mom vacuuming my room in one of her psychotic cleaning episodes. Meaning, instead of letting me clean my room by myself, she busts in and her head explodes because she cannot handle the squalor in which her daughter lives, and proceeds to run a vacuum over every surface. Including my teddy bear, Sir Buster. RUDE! And she does this while yelling a self-pitying monologue the entire time that somehow implicates both my sister and me as the Worst Daughters to Have Ever Lived.

So, my mother asking suspiciously about my shower in the middle of the afternoon was the last straw. It was the last straw in one crappy haystack of a day. A haystack mixed with poop.

I quickly put on some clothes and did my hair. (How I "do my hair": flip head upside down and vigorously towel dry. Rub some gooey stuff from a jar onto palms and run through hair until it looks messy and fun. Done.)

I decided to call David to see what he was up to — I needed to escape.

"What up, Hizzle."

"Hey, D. Can we do something today?"

"Vague much?"

"ANYTHING! My parents are this close to dying by the hand of their firstborn."

"Tell me about it. My dad lectured me about my music again today."

David plays the guitar and is in a band with Carrie — the Raw Meat Demons. Anyway, his dad really hates on his music. He thinks it takes too much time away from his "studies." Which is ridiculous because David doesn't need to study one second of his life to ace all his tests. Which, by the way, is really annoying to someone who crams all night to get a B-minus on a geometry quiz.

"Well, let's plan an escape. Want to hit the beach?" I asked.

"Nah, it's cold now."

"Okay then. A movie?"

"I just spent my last dollar on new strings."

"Ugh. You're so annoying."

"*You're* annoying. Let's just go to Marty's, then."

"Nuh-uh. Too close. Next." Marty's is the used bookstore in Pacific Beach. I usually love it, but it's only like two minutes away from my house.

"Hiz, you can't shoot down all my ideas."

"What? That was only one idea. And you're shooting down MINE first!"

"Jeeeeez-uh. Let's call Carrie and Liz and see what they think."

A few minutes later I was heading out to meet up with everyone at the Burrito Shack. But, of course, as I was pulling on my shoes in the foyer, my dad ambled by.

"Oh!" He halted in front of me. "Where are you going, Holly?"

I didn't make eye contact with him. Making eye contact is the quickest way to get roped into some chore or another.

"I'm going to get lunch with my friends."

"Lunch? With who?"

Okay, seriously. My dad acts like this every single time I say I'm doing anything, as if the idea of having lunch with friends is as surprising as me declaring I was moving out.

"Daaad! With Carrie, Elizabeth, and David. *Who else?*"

My mother chose that moment to pop her head into the foyer and squawk, "Why are you yelling at your dad?"

My sister stuck her head in, too. "Hey, how come Holly doesn't have to clean her room? No faaaair."

Steam was literally, *literally* pouring out my ears.

"I'M NOT YELLING! I'M GOING TO EAT LUNCH! AND THEN PROCEED TO KILL BABIES!"

Mom glared at me. "That mouth of yours gets worse every day! Who speaks that way to her own parents?"

Dad chimed in. "Why do you have to go out to eat lunch with your friends? Are you rich? Do you not have a family? You should eat here at your own house!"

All three of them were now looking at me expectantly.

"Oh. My. GOD."

With that, I ran out the door and hopped onto my bike, pedaling down the street with murderous rage propelling me at record speeds.

I knew I'd get another earful when I got home, but at the moment I just needed to escape before my clothes were ripped off by the huge green muscles that might grow spontaneously from my body.

I pulled up to the Burrito Shack to see that Carrie and David were already seated outside with their bikes parked in front. I locked up my seafoam-green cruiser and jogged over to them.

Carrie took one look at my face and said, "Let me guess. Your parents were *super* excited you were coming out to meet us!"

I plopped down on a seat next to her and across from David. "Don't even get me started. I am counting the days until I can graduate and leave that prison."

David placed his elbows on the table and leaned in toward me. "Aren't you being a *tad* overdramatic here? It can't be that bad."

Before I could open my mouth to school him, a BMW and a Porsche squealed up in front of us, sending exhaust straight into our faces. People piled out of the two cars, making a huge scene — girls in their up-the-butt shorts and thousand-dollar handbags, guys in their aviator shades and popped collars. Leading the pack was Matthew Reynolds, water polo captain and popular kid extraordinaire. In other words, the BEST GROUP OF PEOPLE EVER!

"Slumming it at the Burrito Shack, I see," I said, turning my back to them.

"Yeah, what the heck, this is *our* place. No burritos in La Jolla?" Carrie muttered. La Jolla was an exclusive beach town just north of us, and most of the insufferable rich jock brains usually hung out there.

"Even the lamest among us know where to find the best burritos," David said lazily, propping his bubbly skater shoes up onto the bench next to me.

I pushed them off and stood up reluctantly. "Did you guys order already?" They nodded, so I walked over to wait in line by myself. I stood behind two girls in Matthew's crew, a petite, overly tan brunette named Jessica and a blonde named Megan with a severe case of bitchface.

"I'm not really into the Barneys sale. All it does is bring out all the Chinese hordes hunting for discounted jeans," said Megan.

I held my tongue and resisted the urge to poke the girl in the eyes. Instead, I cleared my throat loudly to let my Asian presence be known. They barely noticed me. How did they know I wasn't Chinese? The fact of the matter is, they didn't *care*. I didn't even exist to them.

I was fuming by the time I ordered my California burrito (a delicious masterpiece of carne asada — marinated beef — French fries, and guacamole. Holy heart attack in a tortilla!). As I headed toward my seat, I heard a low wolf whistle behind me. I turned around to see Elizabeth closing the door on her red Mini Cooper, sending a glare to the guys in Matthew's crew.

One of them, a particularly overly buff football player named Roderick, yelled out, "You gonna call a *jihad*?" then started chanting an exaggerated, high-pitched "Ai yi yi yi yi yi!" The other two guys with him burst into laughter, *dude*ing and high-fiving like mad. Matthew seemed to be ignoring the entire scene, looking at his phone while sitting with Megan and Jessica, who were taking photos of each other with pursed lips. Liz walked over to us, ignoring the chanting.

"Do you want me to kill them?" David asked as he popped a tortilla chip into his mouth. Nothing about his lethargic posture indicated murderous capabilities.

"Oh, let *me*!" said Carrie, her face already turning red.

The chanting grew louder and louder. Other customers were staring at them, but it didn't seem to bother them that much.

"Are you f-ing KIDDING ME?" I shouted over the noise.

"SHUT UP!" Carrie bellowed.

I looked over at Liz, who was applying a coat of lip gloss, seemingly nonplussed by what was happening. David was also silent, but I could see him twirling his straw between his fingers — something David only did when he was pissed but keeping it in. Even though he might not show it, I know he hated this group of guys more than all of us did combined.

A loud whistle pierced through the noise and the chanting stopped abruptly. I craned my neck to see Matthew standing with his hands up. "All right, everyone, chill." With that, he put his aviators back on and sat down. Jessica draped her arm over him possessively and purred, "Good job, Matty." He shrugged her off and bit into his burrito. After one last "Ai yi!" from Roderick, the other guys jostled each other as they finally joined Matthew and the girls.

"I've lost my appetite. Let's go somewhere else," I said, shoving my barely touched burrito away from me.

"Yeah, this place has officially been tainted by a huge infiltration of SUCK," David announced loudly.

Liz just shrugged. "It's cool, you guys. They're idiots. Like bratty little children, they'll stop their bad behavior if you ignore them."

"Or if their god, Matthew, shuts them up?" Carrie said, furiously chomping on her bean-and-cheese burrito.

"They're just so *entitled*. Who thinks it's okay to act like that in public? I'm *over* it!" I seethed.

As if my pestering family wasn't enough, my day was now further ruined by a group of spoiled brats who only cared about which Barneys sale had the least amount of Chinese customers.

"I can't wait for this weekend to be over," I muttered.

NINE

. . . .

UNEXPECTED BARF INCIDENT
BRINGS ENEMIES TOGETHER

I watched Amir Kattan barf onto his computer.

"Ohhhh, nooooo, man," he groaned. My instinct was to scream and run in the opposite direction, but Amir — our usually virile and overly testosteroned sports editor — looked seriously ill.

"Err . . . don't worry, Amir, I'll make sure it gets cleaned. You should probably go to the nurse's office though, yeah?" I patted his back awkwardly and tried not to breathe in through my nose.

As other people in the journalism room noticed what had happened they either ran to get paper towels or doubled over in laughter. Nice. Mr. Williams walked Amir to the nurse's office, sending everyone a stern look as he headed out.

I tried to continue copyediting a riveting article on the new cafeteria supervisor, but it was difficult to concentrate with fresh barf scent lingering on the desk next to mine. Oh, yes, and it was hard to copyedit when I kept dozing off after reading each sentence of this boring piece of crap.

"Hey, Holly."

Ugh. Isabel. The last time she came over to me with that cloying voice I almost got suspended.

"Yes?"

She pushed her wire-framed glasses up on her nose. "So, I don't think Amir is coming back for a few days. Mr. Williams just called and said Amir's been fighting off the stomach flu or something."

Ew. Note to self: disinfect workstation and spray down entire body with Purell.

"Anyway, he's on deadline for a big feature we're doing on Matthew Reynolds. Soooo, since you're working on your last copyediting piece, I'm going to have you take over the assignment."

I groaned. "MATTHEW REYNOLDS?"

Isabel rolled her eyes. "Yes, Matthew Reynolds. You know, all-American football player, captain of the water polo team, and BHS leading point guard?"

"I know who he is. And, no offense, but no thanks."

"Holly, we all know you hate him. But he's also a star athlete and we've been planning this feature for weeks. So, no offense, but you're doing the story."

I frowned as deeply as humanly possible. "Fine. When's the deadline and how long does it have to be?"

"Um, the deadline is actually this Friday and it has to be a thousand words."

I blinked. "Pardon me?"

"Just do it. He was supposed to meet Amir after school today so he could interview him at home."

"HIS home?"

"Yes. Oh yeah, and don't forget to mention Thanksgiving somehow. Get a glowing picture of how ridiculously wholesome and American his family is by describing their Thanksgiving dinner or something. Good luck, bye-bye." She skipped away, her neon-yellow Reeboks squeaking along the tile floor.

I stared at Isabel's back as I thought of the incident with Matthew's friends at the Burrito Shack. Why in the world did I ever decide to work for *The Weasel Times?*

"C'mon, Carrie! Just this once!"

Carrie turned her back to Liz. "No! I am not letting you give me a pedicure. Gross, no way will I ever let another human touch my feet."

"You know what's gross? The state of your toenails," Liz said, pointing a French-tipped fingernail at Carrie's feet.

"Dude, Holly, get this psycho off my back. Let's go to D's house and play Wii Sports Resort!" Carrie exclaimed. It was after school and we were all standing outside BHS's entrance.

David skated around me in circles. (He does this sometimes to make me motion sick.) "Yeah, Hizzle, we need a Speed Slice rematch!"

I nervously searched for the unmistakable jockish hulk that was Matthew Reynolds. "Um, yeah, can't make it today, guys. You will not believe it, but I have to hang out with Matthew Reynolds today to write a story on His Douchiness."

Both Liz and Carrie made faces, and David stopped in his tracks, almost falling off his skateboard. "WHAT?"

"I know. This is torture." I lowered my voice to a whisper in case he or any of his minions were around. "I have to go to his house."

Liz looked horrified. "OMG. Please don't touch anything or you might come back with an STD."

David snickered. "Or worse. You may come back stupider."

"I hear he like, has his own 'suite' for getting it on with girls," Carrie said in a hushed voice. "His parents like, built it for him."

I shuddered. "Well, I'll scream if we go anywhere near a bedroom."

David scowled and fixed his beanie. "Why does this guy need an entire article written about him anyway? High schools always glorify these idiot jocks — reinforcing the idea that high school sports actually matter in life. In a few years these lameoids will be fat and unhappily married with no job skills."

Liz poked him jokingly. "As opposed to the job skills you get from *skating?*"

"Well, that's just cool. When I'm old, I'll just be cool."

At that moment, I spotted Matthew.

Walking with his usual entourage of bitchez and arses,

he was about a head taller than everyone else. His dark blond hair was perfectly tousled, a very groomed surfer look. Wearing a crisp white button-down with the sleeves rolled up and a pair of navy blue shorts that fit *just so*, he looked every bit the privileged little San Diego teen. He even had the walk perfected — this lazy swagger with a puffed chest. He was so assured in knowing that the world was his oyster. How does one get to be so ridiculously full of oneself? Maybe I'd bring him down a notch.

"See you guys later," I said mournfully, and gave one last glance to my three best friends, who all looked like they were sending me off to the electric chair.

I walked up to Matthew, and bitchface Megan standing by him stopped midsentence to throw me a disgusted look. I threw a nasty one right back at her. Hell if I was going to let these people get to me again.

"Matty, uh, someone's here to see you, I think," Roderick said in his nasally prepster voice. Everyone stared at me and some even snickered. Really? Are we in the freaking seventh grade again?

"Why do you look familiar to me? Oh yeah, the one with the hot friend. Ai yi yi!" said Roderick with a sharp bark of laughter. Douche.

"She's so *not* hot. More like tacky *Shahs of Sunset* material," Jessica, the future skin cancer patient, said.

The words flew out of my mouth before I could stop them. "Better that than *Jersey Shore*, Snooki," I said.

All chatting stopped and everyone stared at me. Why was I messing with these people? They were the kind of evil high school villains who would douse my head in pig's blood without a second thought.

The silence was suddenly interrupted by a choked laugh. I looked up in surprise at Matthew, who was turning red behind a fist that unsuccessfully hid a smile.

Jessica pouted and tugged on his arm. "Matty, are you going to let her talk to me like that?"

"You started it," I said under my breath.

Matthew removed her hand and looked at me. "Sooo, can I help you with something?"

My momentary bravado left me and I got super self-conscious, patting down my messy crop of hair and adjusting my backpack. This was my first time talking to Matthew even though I'd gone through elementary and middle school with him. And even though I made fun of him endlessly and was disgusted by his mere existence, it was a little terrifying to be the object of his attention, no matter how briefly.

"Yeah, um, I'm taking over the *Weasel Times* story. Amir's sick," I said, trying to feign nonchalance.

Matthew raised an eyebrow. "You? Aren't you the one with that like, little column?"

"Little Miss Big Mouth. Don't say much in person, though, huh?" Roderick said with a sneer that would make James Spader proud.

Do not resort to violence. Do not resort to violence.

Anger and humiliation were clouding my vision, so I turned around instinctively, looking for my friends. They were gone. I bit my lip — I was in this alone.

"Your friends left, honey," Jessica said with a smile.

I was through with this hilarious popular-kids-versus-me banter. "Can we just get this over with?"

Matthew looked at me with slight disbelief. "Wow, rude much?"

"Uh, have you MET your friends?" I responded with lightning-quick speed.

He yawned a few inches away from my face. Without covering his mouth. Who does this guy think he IS? "Whatever, man."

He grunted a few good-byes to his friends, who were openly glaring at me, then said, "Now what?"

"Um . . . your house, I think?" I said, almost cringing.

"Right. I'll drive."

Of course he would.

TEN

. . . .

THE MATTHEW REYNOLDS STORY

Shoving my body as close to the car door as humanly possible, I peered out the window at the huge houses we were driving past. Of course this is where he would live. We were riding through a super exclusive beach community — many of the houses were gated and hidden behind huge expanses of lawns and trees.

The ten-minute drive had been excruciating. He'd blasted Linkin Park and Fall Out Boy, and it took every ounce of my willpower to refrain from smashing his iPhone to smithereens.

"All right, we're here," he announced with zero enthusiasm as we pulled into a gated driveway and parked directly at his doorstep.

My jaw dropped. His house was enormous. But that wasn't the surprising part, as I didn't doubt for a moment that a d-bag like Matthew would live in some mansion. But it was actually really cool — modern with glass walls and beautiful wood panels. I had imagined some tacky columned fortress.

"Uh, wow. Cool house," I managed to eek out.

He shrugged (seriously — was he capable of any other gesture in LIFE?) and walked toward the house, keys loosely dangling in his hand. "I guess. It's good for parties."

Matthew was also notorious for his ragers — people always talked about them like he was Hugh Hefner. I, obviously, had never been to one. Why would I ever want to do such a thing?

We entered through a massive door that blended seamlessly into the house, and I stood in the entrance gawking for a bit. The entire west side of the place was paneled in glass and the Pacific spread out as far as the eye could see.

"Wow." I didn't know how else to articulate myself.

He sauntered over to the kitchen, which was just kind of floating in the middle of the living area. "You want something to drink?"

It was an oddly polite question. But again, I'm sure he was used to being a host. "Okay, what do you have?"

He opened the stainless-steel refrigerator door wide open in response. It was completely filled with beverages. Sodas, beer, juices, sparkling water — you name it.

"Whoa. I guess some apple juice?" I wasn't even thirsty but everything looked so delicious and pristine.

He pulled out a bottle and poured it into a glass for me. I took it awkwardly. "Thanks. So, where's all the food? Do you have a separate fridge for it or something?"

"Nah. We don't really have food — I mostly order in stuff. Or eat out."

"Wow, your family eats out every night?!"

"No, I do."

"By yourself?"

He took a generous swig of sparkling water before answering. "Yeeeah. Yup."

Weird. "Don't your parents make you eat with them?"

"Uhhh, nope. They're not home too much."

I laughed. "Lucky."

He threw me a peculiar look. "I guess."

"Can I get a tour of the house? Do you mind if I take pictures for the article?" I held up the *Weasel Times*' digital camera.

"Oh, yeah, sure."

I followed him as he walked me through the sprawling house, snapping pictures here and there. I tried to get some info on the house, on his family, but it was like talking to a wall. While not particularly hateful, Matthew was proving to be completely boring.

"Who built this house? It looks like a lot of care went into the design."

"Uh . . . I don't know. Some architect my dad knows."

"Are these floors made out of bamboo?"

"I think so."

"Wow, are those all solar panels?"

"Yep."

I pointed to a photo of a ruggedly handsome man in a suit and a beautiful woman in a dress with 1980s-style shoulder pads. "Are these your parents?"

"Yep."

PLEASE, THE ENTHUSIASM WAS OVERWHELMING.

"Well, should we start the interview, then?" I asked as we walked back to the kitchen. I was praying he would give me more details and personality. This was going awkwardly as hell.

He shrugged again, pulling out a chair and propping his legs up onto the pristine, white breakfast tabletop. I positioned a chair across from him, making sure to keep a sizable distance between us. If there's one thing I can't stand, it's people having a good view of my pores in the harsh daylight. *Especially* if "people" is someone who purportedly dates only bathing suit models with perfect poreless skin. He had probably never even seen a zit before. I scanned my list of questions. "All right, so . . . maybe first we can just talk about the usual stats. Where you were born, what your parents do and all that?" I asked while setting up the digital recorder.

He picked up my pen and started fiddling with it, not looking at me. A few seconds passed and he cleared his throat. "I don't know. . . . Does anyone really care about that?"

"Yessss," I replied testily. His total lack of interest in this interview couldn't be more evident, from his lazy-bum pose to his bored rich-boy face.

He closed his eyes from the sheer exhaustion of having to speak to me. "I was born on a cold winter's day in 1996."

I glared at him, hoping my silence spoke volumes. How would I tell Isabel that I had no story because Matthew Reynolds was the most boring jock to have ever attended Bay High?

At that moment the back door into the kitchen slammed open and a little girl flew in, all blond braids and giant backpack. She threw the backpack on the floor and ran over to the next room, all without acknowledging our presence.

Matthew grinned widely and called out, "Hey, Amelia!" She looked up from under the coffee table where she was inspecting a large stuffed carrot, then made eye contact with me. She immediately buried her face in the carrot and turned away from us.

I tried to laugh it off. "Kids love me." Matthew looked apologetic, but before he could speak a Latina woman wearing a hoodie and yoga pants walked in, carrying an armload of bags. Matthew shot over to take them from her. She gave him a grateful smile and squeezed his shoulder. "Thanks, kiddo." She noticed me and smiled curiously.

"Carina, this is Holly, she's a reporter for the school paper doing a story on me. Holly, this is Carina, Amelia's nanny."

Carina walked over to me and shook my hand. "How wonderful! Nice to meet you, Holly." She shot me another warm smile and then turned to Matthew. "The teacher said Amelia managed to nap today so she should be okay for the rest of the evening. And she did this in class today, which is a huge deal." She held up a large piece of paper with a drawing of a rainbow-striped horse.

Matthew's eyes widened. "Wow! That's great."

"And, Matty, I'm so sorry to interrupt your interview, but do you think you can take over for a while? I just got a call from my oldest saying she needs a ride to her swim lesson. I'll be back in time for dinner."

"Of course," Matthew said without hesitation. Carina looked relieved. "Thank you! Also, here's the paperwork from the center that your parents need to sign."

He rolled his eyes. "Yeah, right."

Carina gave him a sympathetic look. "You're a good boy. I'll see you soon." She turned to me and waved. "Nice meeting you, Holly! Bye, Amelia, I'll be right back!" she called out. No response from Amelia, but Carina didn't seem to mind. She gave us a final wave and closed the door.

"She seems nice," I replied, kind of dazed by this entire scene. The Matthew I was seeing now was completely different from the one who had been lazily answering questions earlier.

"Sorry, I need to make Amelia a snack. Would you mind keeping an eye on her for a sec?" he asked as he dug around the cupboards.

"Sure," I replied, sitting up straighter to be more alert even though Amelia was directly in my line of vision, this time in the middle of the family room. In fact, she was crouched into a little ball now, rocking back and forth on her heels, keeping her carrot close to her.

He arranged some graham crackers on a plate, then made frustrated noises as he looked through the fridge. "You'd think we'd have a piece of fruit or something in this stupid house." He managed to scrounge out an apple, carefully sliced it into pieces, and spread some peanut butter onto each slice.

"Amelia Smelly-lia, it's snack time!" he hollered.

Silence. Matthew sighed. "Be right back." He walked over to her and knelt down, but she shrieked in response. Matthew started shushing her, but she got louder, until she was full-on screaming at the top of her lungs.

I sat there uncomfortably. Should I be doing something?

Just when I was about to get up and go see if he needed help, the screaming stopped. "Time to eat, okay? Let's go in the kitchen," he cajoled her. She reluctantly got up and followed closely behind. I noticed that during this entire interaction the two had never touched. "Okay, snack time for the little monkey."

The teeniest of smiles hovered on Amelia's lips as she pulled herself up onto a stool alongside the granite kitchen counter.

Matthew handed her an apple slice. She shook her head. He placed it on the plate and she picked it up herself and munched on it.

"Don't forget the yummy juice," he said as he held it up to her, a colorful coiled straw tempting her. She took a long drag and then pulled away. They continued to do this until the straw rattled with the sound of an empty cup.

She eventually hopped off and ran into the family room again. "Would you mind if we did this in the other room until Carina gets back?"

"Yeah, yeah of course, no problem," I said hurriedly, grabbing my stuff. Matthew leaned over and took everything from me.

"Here, let me," he said, smoothly swinging my backpack over one arm. Wait, what?

"Oh, um, okay. Thanks." Flustered, I followed him into the family room.

Amelia was sitting in front of the wall of windows, staring out at the ocean. I stood next to her to see what she was looking at, but there was nothing apart from the ocean and the jacaranda trees moving in the breeze on their deck. I smiled and looked down at her. "Anything interesting out there?"

Barely a flicker of acknowledgment of my presence. She didn't answer, and I felt oddly sheepish, like I was interrupting the deep thoughts of a four-year-old.

"Don't be offended, she's not ignoring you on purpose," Matthew said. He was sitting on the floor, leaning against a sofa.

I walked over and sat down across from him, spreading out my notes and recording equipment. "Oh, it's fine. . . . I mean, kids actually don't love me."

He lowered his voice. "Well, she's different from most kids. Um, she's autistic?"

"Oh! Oh, okay!"

I had no idea how to react. I am the worst reactor to

serious things. Am I supposed to say "Sorry"? Isn't that insulting? Because you don't have to be all feeling sorry for someone with an autistic sibling. That seems so condescending. But "Rad!" didn't feel like the appropriate response either.

Matthew looked at me curiously. "Oh, do you know what it is?"

I got super self-conscious again and wanted to avert the Matthew Reynolds gaze away from me. Preferably with all my hair covering my face.

"Yeah! I mean, but I'm not like, an expert. . . . I just, know what it is? Kind of?" Words were just barfing a mile a minute out of my mouth.

"Oh, cool. Most people aren't that familiar with it." Matthew started talking really quickly, too. He sat up straighter and was the most animated I'd ever seen him. "But Amelia does really well with her therapy, and she's pretty high functioning even though she's only four years old."

"Well, I mean, I didn't really think anything was that off. I mean, you know what I mean," I said awkwardly.

Before Matthew could respond to that highly intelligent comment, the front door opened and high heels clicked across the wood floors.

"Hello?" a woman's singsongy voice called out.

"We're in here!" Matthew yelled.

A woman who was an older version of the 1980s hottie in the photo I saw earlier walked into the room, bringing a cloud of expensive perfume with her. She was tall, slim, and her dark blond hair was perfectly highlighted and curled. Matthew clearly got his cheekbones from this woman.

"Matthew, my goodness, your car needs a wash!" she said before giving him an air kiss. Huh? Matthew's ridiculous Porsche was spotless. He shrugged in response.

I stood up halfway to greet her, but she pulled out her crystal-encrusted phone and started texting.

I sat there kind of uneasily. Hello?

She eventually finished her text and walked over to Amelia and ruffled her hair. "Hi there, princess!" Amelia shook her off with a screech and started rocking back and forth on her heels again. Matthew's mom frowned for a moment, then put on a bright smile again, looking at her reflection in the sliding doors.

Matthew finally spoke up. "Hey, Mom, this is Holly. She's writing a story on me for *The Weasel Times*."

I stood up again, not sure what the protocol was with this glamorous woman. "Hi, Mrs. Reynolds. Nice to meet you."

Her darkly lined green eyes widened and she immediately shot me a big smile. "Hi there, dear! An article on our Matty! How lovely."

Before I could say anything, her phone rang shrilly. She fumbled around the pockets of her cashmere camel coat and picked it up, smiling already. "Oh, hi, Sylvie! Yes, I was just about to call you about it. Can you believe it?" She walked back toward the front door of the house, calling out over her shoulder, "Bye, dears. Matty, don't forget Daddy and I are out to Mexico for the weekend. Make sure you remind Carina!" And with that, she was out of the house again, her scent lingering in the air.

It took me a moment to register what Mrs. Reynolds had just said. "Your parents are going to Mexico for Thanksgiving?"

"Yup."

"But you're not? And Amelia's not?"

"Nah."

"So you're going to spend Thanksgiving alone?"

He laughed. "You make it sound so messed up. I haven't spent Thanksgiving with my parents in like, years. They love to travel for the holidays. I like being home, so it's cool."

While the idea of spending a holiday blissfully alone, away from my chaotic family, did sound tempting, it also felt wrong somehow. But Matthew didn't seem to mind.

He glanced at his watch. "Should we continue the interview?"

I almost forgot why I was there in the first place. "Yes, thanks for reminding me!"

So with Amelia playing quietly by herself, I continued to ask a way more relaxed and cooperative Matthew Reynolds questions. By the time six rolled around, I had a ton of information for the article.

"Thanks, Matthew. Hopefully this shapes up to be a decent profile. It'll be my first one," I said.

"Well, this is my first profile, too. So I guess we're all good?" he said with a smile. I couldn't help but smile back at him.

My cell phone beeped. I looked down to see a text from Ann: "Momz going to kill u if you don't get home soon. LOL."

My parents *would* kill me if I was even a minute late. They had been psychotically on my case ever since the local news started incessantly reporting a story on some man in a van kidnapping children. I repeat, children. Sigh.

"Sorry, but I have to get home now. Can you drop me off, or do you have to wait for Carina?" I asked.

Matthew grabbed his keys off the counter and said, "No worries. Amelia does really well in cars."

As we drove, Amelia quietly chatted to herself in the backseat. When we got to Pacific Beach, I asked Matthew to drop me off a few blocks away from my house.

"Uh, are you sure you don't want to be dropped off closer?" he asked, looking dubiously at the group of skater kids who were glaring at us from a storefront.

"Oh, yeah. If my parents saw your car pull up — oh my God, they'd be so annoying."

"Those guys look shady."

I waved my hand dismissively. "They're just the stoner losers that hang out here every day. They're ugly, but essentially harmless." He let out a sharp bark of laughter and I looked at him in surprise. I felt oddly pleased that I could make the Blasé King laugh.

Amelia let out a copycat bark of laughter, which made all of us crack up. "You're kinda funny, Holly K.," Matthew said.

I blushed. Like, blushed. "Um, thanks."

And then there was this moment. A blink-and-you'll-miss-it moment. He kind of tilted his head and looked at me. My blushing was out of control at this point and I could barely look at him. And you know what? He WAS good-looking. I mean, I always knew it, similar to the way everyone knows Brad Pitt is good-looking. But I didn't give a crap about how good-looking Brad Pitt was because he always struck me as boring as hell.

"What?" I asked, because he was still staring at me.

He looked down into his lap. "Well, I was just thinking."

My heart skipped a beat. What was wrong with me?! Was I getting a crush on MATTHEW F-ING REYNOLDS?

"Yes?" I asked, my voice kind of cracking. This was an oddly romantic-comedy moment. And my life? Is not a romantic comedy. It is just pure comedy. It's *Curb Your Enthusiasm* as an Asian American girl.

He sighed heavily. "So, are you going to include everything in this article?"

I blinked. Oh.

"Er, ummmm, I don't know. I mean . . ." See, as a journalist, you can't promise anyone anything. In the end, you can write whatever the heck you want because technically you are not held accountable to anyone. Other than your boss, maybe.

My lame answer elicited the familiar shrug. The wall had come back down.

"Never mind. Write whatever you want. Forget I said anything."

He was staring out the window now, and I looked at him for a moment. "Okay." Silence. "Thanks for the ride."

"You're welcome," he automatically said. Polite till the end.

I said bye to Amelia, got out of the car, and closed the door. I stood there not knowing what to do for a moment, and then waved. He waved back. I started walking, and thought he would zoom away. But when I glanced back, there he was in the same spot, Porsche idling. He was glaring at the skaters.

That night, after Ann and I went through our usual sparring over the dishes, I sat down in front of my laptop to check my Facebook page. I almost knocked over my green tea when I saw that Matthew Reynolds had posted on my wall:

Hope you liked the apple juice.

My face grew hot. This could not be happening to me. Please, God, pleasepleaseplease don't let me have a crush on Matthew Reynolds. MATTHEW F-ING REYNOLDS.

But, it was just so darn cute. I mean, why did he leave that post? Didn't he care that everyone else in the world would see that he, Matthew F-ing Reynolds, left a post for me, Holly F-ing Kim?

I closed the browser window before I could do anything foolish — like leave a responding comment on his post. After some quick Internet stalking, I found that his profile was covered in a billion comments from girls. Bleugh.

Instead, I decided to blast the new Muse album and start my Matthew Reynolds article. I looked through my notes and decided to begin the piece with Matthew's story about his first Little League game.

The rest of the story followed easily, practically flowing through my fingers. I typed furiously — about his childhood, his fisherman grandpa, his Swedish scientist grandmother, his junior high sports stardom, his trips to Africa and Europe.

I wrote about everything but his parents. I wrote about how cool his house was, the view, the many rooms. I also mentioned his cute little sister, but as a side note. I steered clear of any autism talk.

As I reread the story, I realized I was missing the all-American heartwarming slant that Isabel wanted. Something about Thanksgiving. I remembered his mom's space-cadet reminder about her trip to Mexico. A trip without her kids, one of whom had special needs. What was Matthew going to do by himself with his four-year-old sister while everyone else was spending Thanksgiving with family?

No, I decided to not write about Matthew's parents or his secret: that he was almost single-handedly raising an autistic sister in a big, empty house.

ELEVEN

SOURCES SAY SECRET TO THE PERFECT THANKSGIVING MEAL IS KIMCHI

Is THAT YOU, HOLLY?"

I sighed. "Noooo, it's the Van Rapist."

"Rapist! *Omo*, I don't know how you think of such horrible things. I must have had too much spicy food while pregnant with you," I heard her mutter from the kitchen.

I laughed. "Nothing like kimchi to spawn the child of the devil!"

It was Thanksgiving at the Kim household, and it was absolute mayhem, the weekly Kim dinner on steroids. All my extended family happened to live in Southern California, so holidays were extra jam-packed — everyone drove out from their various suburbs to land at the family of choice. This year, that family was ours.

The kitchen was filled to the brim with women — five at the stove, three to a tiny one-foot counter space, knives and cutting boards spread with a variety of meats and vegetables. I could barely tell one aunt from the next through the steam billowing from pots and pans. The men were outside in the backyard, lounging around with beers, half-heartedly attempting to help my dad grill.

My grandparents and some of the younger kids were in the family room, the older women talking over tea while the kids screeched and slammed toys into each other's bodies. The majority of my older cousins were packed like sardines into the living room, some watching a football game on TV, others on their laptops or sitting around and chatting.

I walked into the kitchen holding a grocery bag. "I got the potatoes. Where should I put them?" Mandy and Danny's mom quickly took them from my hands and started scrubbing them furiously in the sink. "You're welcome!" I called to no one in particular.

"Holly, you kids should start setting the tables!" my mom said. She was sitting on the kitchen floor, grating turnips.

I corralled some cousins and we expanded the dining room table, inserting the extra leaves so that it doubled in size. Then we went to the garage and pulled out our folding tables and chairs.

"Ew, these are disgusting," I said from one end of a table as my entire shirt got covered in dust and grime. On the other side, my cousin Danny blew on the table and even more dust flew into my face. I dropped the table and ran after him. "You're dead!" I yelled as he bolted across the front lawn.

My mom was watching from the doorway. "Clean them before you bring them in!"

Ugh. I was filthy and my cousins were rolling in the grass in laughter. I babysat these brats for most of my life, and I had to show them I was still the boss. I grabbed the hose lying on the front lawn and started drenching everyone in sight.

Ann squealed and ran off to hide behind a bush. "Now YOU'RE dead!" Danny called as he nosedived behind a car in the driveway. I managed to spray him on the butt before he went out of sight.

I was wheezing from laughing so hard, and then felt cold water drench me from above. "Oh my GOD!" I yelped. Sputtering, I turned to see Mark and Mandy behind me holding a huge empty bucket, both of them soaking wet, too. Before I could exact my revenge, my mom's voice pierced through the chaos.

"HOLLY HEE-YOUNG KIM!"

Everyone froze. I looked up to see my mom looking furious beyond words. She had busted out my full name. She was maaaaad.

"What is wrong with you? You're one of the oldest kids here and THIS is the example you're setting? GET INSIDE. NOW."

Everyone shuffled inside, trying to keep a straight face. "Go inside now or clean up the table and chairs first?" I asked angrily, wiping water out of my eyes.

She looked torn — what was more important, cracking down on me or clean tables and chairs? Cleanliness won out in the end. "Clean them first!" she barked, and then went into the house, slamming the door behind her.

My cousins sheepishly came back outside to help me wipe down the furniture, and then we hauled it inside, where the uncles finally got off their butts to set it up for us.

I dried off in the bathroom, squeezing in between Mandy and Katie. "Pass me the blow-dryer!" I shouted over the noise. Katie handed it to me and we jostled for mirror space, giggling the entire time.

When we finally joined everyone for dinner, the tables were already set out — the kids' table separate from the adults', as always. Laid out on them was a delicious hybrid of traditional American Thanksgiving fare (minus the gross marshmallows that Americans like to put on top of their yams) and Korean food. Among the platters of turkey, stuffing, and cranberries were small dishes of kimchi, marinated ribs, and noodles with vegetables.

"Shall we say grace?" my cousin James said in a high-pitched voice, and the kids cracked up. Everyone had started digging into the food already. There was no saying of grace or any real discussion of what we were thankful for, but I think our thanks was evident enough as we dug into our food with gusto — happily chewing in silence. I looked around at my large family. They definitely annoyed the heck out of me but I couldn't imagine a Thanksgiving without them.

* * *

Have I ever mentioned how disgusting my locker is? Every time I open it, I'm like, "Something needs to be done." Seriously. There's some sticky substance coating the entire top shelf, there are always crumbs getting into my books, and the dreamy picture I have of Joseph Gordon-Levitt is always falling onto the floor when I slam the door shut.

I was standing there contemplating hosing it down with bleach when I felt a tap on my shoulder.

Well, my goodness. There was Matthew.

"Hey, Holly."

I smiled automatically. "Hey!"

He was holding up the latest issue of *The Weasel Times*. "Cool article."

"Oh, thanks. So you liked it?"

He grinned and did that head-tilt thing again. "It was all right. If you like stories about awesome dudes."

I rolled my eyes. "Nice."

"No, but seriously. Um, thanks for the nice piece. I wasn't really sure what to expect. You know, with your rep and all."

Embarrassed, I pretended to rummage around in my locker for something. "Well, I just wrote the truth."

He gave a slight smile and said, "Right, Holly K. See you around, then." And with that, he was gone in the sea of kids — blond head bobbing higher than most.

Because of my flustered state, I didn't notice that Liz, Carrie, and David were all standing a few feet away from me, slack-jawed. "Hey, guys." I waved feebly at them and they slowly walked over to me.

"Are you like, FRIENDS with Matthew Reynolds now?" Liz gasped, her expression beyond incredulous.

Carrie shook her head so hard that her hair flew around her face and her beaded turquoise earrings jangled loudly. "No way!"

David just stood there looking at me oddly, his hands tucked into skinny jeans that were in danger of falling off his narrow hips.

"Calm down! Geez, you'd think I just hooked up with Stalin!"

Liz leaned against the row of lockers and made a face. "Well, we *are* talking about Matthew Reynolds here."

A flash of irritation shot through me. "Okay, not like you guys know him. At all." They all gave me weird looks again.

"What, is he cool now?" David asked sarcastically.

I glared at him. "Shut up."

David flinched and I immediately felt terrible. "Sorry. Just don't be a jerk about it, okay? He wasn't as bad as I thought he'd be."

Liz folded her arms and looked at me. "Yeah, I read the article. Just short of glowing."

"Oh, please," I said dismissively.

"And what was with the BFF action we just saw?" Carrie demanded. "You two looked like, all cozy."

I almost blushed again. "The thing is, he really wasn't that bad. He was kind of a gentleman. And I felt bad for him."

"BAD? Why?!" David demanded.

I was about to tell them about the whole weirdness

with his flaky parents and his responsibility for his sister. But oddly, at the last second I decided not to tell them. It was Matthew's secret, his Achilles' heel. Everyone else knew him as the Golden Boy whose life was perfect, and I didn't want to be the one to expose him.

My friends looked at me expectantly. I shrugged. "He's just not that dumb. I feel bad that everyone thinks he's dumb."

Liz raised an eyebrow. "Let me get this straight: You . . . feel bad . . . because he is unjustly labeled as dumb?"

"Well, yeah, that's a fancy way of putting it," I replied.

The bell rang just then. Carrie and Liz walked away together with their heads bent, whispering. David skated off, throwing one last strange look at me before disappearing from sight. I knew that my friends would continue to give me crap about Matthew — and that they probably didn't really believe my explanation. But for the time being, his secret was safe with me.

LETTERS TO THE EDITOR

Someone needs to get her facts straight about Thanksgiving. It's not a fact that the Pilgrims gave the Indians smallpox. It's never been proven — stop spreading your liberal propaganda!

— BRYCE K., JUNIOR

As suspected, Matthew Reynolds has everything handed to him on a silver platter. Where's the feature on the students who actually do something for the world?! Like, me. I'm a member of PETA and plant trees on weekends. Holly, you sold out!

— IAN G., SENIOR

SMALLPOX IS THE MOST DISGUSTING THING I'VE EVER SEEEEEEEEEEEN!

— LOLA S., FRESHMAN

If I have to read another article about another cafeteria related *anything* I am going to kill myself.

— KATHERINE A., SOPHOMORE

DECEMBER

For many of you, the holidays mean wonderful things: presents, vacations, skiing, family togetherness, Macaulay Culkin, and some kind of ham.

For many of us children of confused immigrants, it means an entirely different thing. Our parents journeyed to the Land of Opportunity to start new lives and to offer their children better futures than the ones to be had back in the Motherland.

But they forgot to learn a few things on the way over:

1. **Allowance? Bah!** Yeah, we don't get these. My parents laughed in my face at the idea of giving me money every week for burritos and books.

2. **Sleepovers? Yeah, right!** Try telling my mom that it's normal for a bunch of girls to get together at night, sleep on the floor, and summon ghosts with a Ouija board.

3. **Santa Claus? Who the . . .** My parents had no idea until it was too late (read: LAST YEAR)

that Americans have this weird tradition of lying to their children about some fat guy who leaves gifts under a tree in the middle of the night.

So for me, the holidays have always meant massive amounts of friends and family visiting from Korea and a whole heap of Korean food. I've grown used to the fact that my parents have their own way of celebrating the holidays. I've maybe grown to like it or something. But knowing that my friends were going on snowboarding trips to Colorado and waking up on Christmas morning to Bing Crosby's holiday hits and piping-hot gingerbread cookies in the oven, I've always kind of wondered what that would be like.

However, this year, my parents revealed a delightful surprise. We're spending Christmas in . . . LAS VEGAS. That's right, the Land of Confused Immigrants who do not understand that Thanksgiving and Christmas don't necessarily correlate with gambling and outlet shopping.

Could there be anything more un-American and depressing? I envy you all.

Viva Las Holidays,

Holly

P.S. Sob.

TWELVE

HOLIDAY DESTINATION FOR KOREANS PUZZLING TO REST OF WORLD

I really love Christmas.

I love the smell of pine trees. I love twinkly lights. I love shopping at breakneck speeds. I love caroling. I love presents. I love *Home Alone*. For someone who is occasionally known as a cynical grump, I can be pretty darn cheerful around the holiday season.

Ann and I were in our gross dust-coated garage digging through boxes in search of our holiday decorations. (I have my suspicions that it's not just dust, but asbestos. Guess we'll find out in a few years when we all grow fins!)

Although my parents pretty much suck with the Christmas décor, they recently discovered the joys of putting up Christmas lights. We were in the middle of untangling them when I heard my mom calling for us.

"WHAT?" I yelled back.

Ann winced. "God, do you have to scream? And why can't Mom just come outside? The whole neighborhood can probably hear her. It's so embarrassing."

Everything was embarrassing to my sister lately. I understood being eleven very well.

"WHAT, MOM?!" What's the point of being older if not to torment those below us?

Ann huffed and glared at me.

"COME INSIDE! DON'T GET THE LIGHTS!"

"Ugh. Let me go see what she wants." I dropped the lights and ran inside. My mom was in the kitchen writing something down on a piece of paper. She looked up when I came in.

"You and Ann don't need to put the lights up this year."

I put my hands on my hips, confused. "Huh? Why not? Is Dad going to do it?" I asked this with some dread. My dad had tried putting up the lights a few times, and each time it involved some sloppy draping between tree limbs and poles. Not only was it ugly, but I thought it posed a serious fire hazard. And my dad has already had a few run-ins with the fire department.

My mom kept her eyes on what she was writing, which looked suspiciously like doodling. "No. We're going on vacation this year!"

Excitement coursed through me. "Really?! Where? New York?" I had pleaded for years to spend Christmas in

New York. On TV the snowy trees in Central Park and ice skating rink at Rockefeller Center always looked magical. I couldn't imagine how amazing they'd be in person.

"Nooo, not New York. You know, my friend, the rich one, in Korea?" Seriously, how many of my mom's announcements have started this way? She continued, "Well, her family is visiting, and they thought it would be really fun to spend Christmas in, you know, Las Vegas."

My mom sped up that last part. And for good reason.

"WHAT?" I asked. My mom ignored me studiously as she continued her doodling.

"Mother! No way! I am not going to Las Vegas for Christmas!"

She finally looked up at me with a warning look. "It'll be fun, you'll see. I don't know what it is with you and Las Vegas anyway. Why don't you like it?"

Oh, let me count the ways. Ever since I was a little kid, I've hated that city. Many Asian American kids from California grow to know it well, as they spend many misguided holidays there. Easter? Egg hunt at the Bellagio! Thanksgiving? The Caesars Palace buffet! Holidays gone terribly, terribly wrong.

If there was one thing my parents got right with the holidays, it was always spending them at home with our extended family. The one or two trips we took to Vegas when I was a child were memorably miserable ones. The heat destroyed me. I spent most of the days reclined lazily across the hotel bed, watching bad movies, two inches away from the air conditioner. And it was so freaking boring. You can do three things in Las Vegas if you're under twenty-one: 1) Eat; 2) Shop; 3) Watch *Legally Blonde* on TV. Everything about the place depressed me. My mother knew this well.

Ann walked in with her usual scowl. "Why are you being so loud? And why aren't we putting up the Christmas lights?"

I looked at her with a shred of hope. Maybe we could unite for once and overcome this obstacle together.

"Guess where we're going for Christmas?" I asked dramatically. A blank, completely disinterested stare looked back at me. "Las Vegas."

She looked at our mom for a second and optimism filled my heart. Then she shrugged and said, "Whatever. Can we see Cirque du Soleil there?"

How this beast person shared my blood was a mystery to me. Feeling utterly betrayed, I walked out without another word and hopped on my bike, headed for Carrie's.

It was a cloudy day, and the air coming off the ocean was especially cold. I rode along Pacific Beach's main thoroughfare, Garnet Avenue, passing all the shoppers, skaters, and hippies that usually crowd the street. I turned left onto Carrie's street and tossed my bike onto her house's front lawn. Her door was wide open as usual and I smelled some kind of nutty bread in the air. Her mom was always baking something with grains.

"Hi, Susan!" I said quickly as I breezed past their kitchen and up the stairs. Even though I've known Carrie and her family since I was five, it still felt strange to call her mom by her first name. If some fifteen-year-old kid tried to call my mom "Mi-Young," I would not want to be within one mile of her.

I found Carrie in her room, a small pile of dusty things on the floor and her feet poking out from underneath her bed. I plopped down on top of it.

"What are you *doing?*"

Carrie stuck her head out to look at me. "Cleaning, what does it look like?"

"Did your parents actually make you clean this weekend?" I asked with surprise. Carrie had always been allowed to keep her room as messy as she wanted it. In fact, her parents were *not allowed in her room without her permission.* I couldn't imagine what my parents' reactions would be if I proposed something similar. Actually, I had a pretty good idea — they'd probably make me sleep in the hallway to teach me a lesson.

"Nah. I just started getting these weird bug bites and thought maybe I should vacuum or something."

I gingerly scooted to the edge of her bed and looked at the bedspread carefully as Carrie stood up and dusted herself off. Gross, dude.

I spotted something colorful sitting on top of the dusty pile. "Hey! Is that the Kachina doll I made for you in fifth grade?!" I asked, excitedly picking up a clay statue wearing a tattered purple sarong and a feather headdress.

"Yup. Good ol' Kachina the Kachina doll."

I looked at her. "Are you kidding? You named her 'Kachina'?"

Carrie shrugged as she grabbed a broom to start sweeping. "Seemed to fit at the time."

"You were always such a creative child."

"Oh, please. Who was the one who named their sex ed egg-baby 'Eggster'?"

I laughed. "Oh, Eggster. Poor Eggster, such a tragic premature egg death."

"I can't believe David sat on her. I still think it was on purpose," Carrie said, plopping down onto a purple bean-bag chair after she tossed the broom aside. She was wearing short overalls and covered in dust, her hair in a sloppy ponytail. Only a select few can get away with wearing overalls and not looking like a four-year-old or a hillbilly. Carrie was one of those people. Although with her dusty strawberry-blond hair and bare feet, she was pulling off hillbilly pretty well.

"So what's up? If I had known you were coming over, I would have pushed the cleaning extravaganza to tomorrow!" she said as she scratched a spot on her ankle. My own ankle started itching in response. This might have to be a quick visit.

"Oh, just came over to share some AWESOME Kim family news."

"God, what now?"

"Guess where my family is going for Christmas?"

She cocked her head to one side. "You guys are going somewhere?"

"Yes. It's an amazing holiday mecca."

"Er, Bethlehem?"

I threw a pillow at her. "NO." I paused dramatically. "Las Vegas."

"Huh? WHY?"

"Because! They don't get American holidays! They don't give a crap about traditions like caroling and . . . and . . . hot cocoa!"

"Hot cocoa?" Carrie asked, confused.

"Whatever. I mean, it's freaking VEGAS! Is it too much to ask that my family be normal and functional just once a year?"

Carrie crossed her legs and leaned forward. "Aren't you being a little overdramatic?"

"NO! Do you even know how many times a year I have to let things slide in my family? Like having no birthday cake, but seaweed soup instead! Art classes? No, no, it's all about Saturday morning math tutorials! You need special glue for your project? No need to waste money — just use sticky rice paste! Cool summer vacation in Hawaii? Why snorkel when you can hike fifty miles on yet another camping trip?!" I could go on, but I stopped because I was starting to sound a little hysterical, even to myself.

Carrie looked at me with pity. "Are you serious? I mean, I know you used to have math classes on Saturdays, but you have to eat seaweed on your birthday?"

Despite my rant, I felt slightly defensive. Seaweed soup was actually one of my favorites. "Well, it's not gross. I'm just saying it's different. But this is the last straw. How in the world can you have a good Christmas in Las Vegas?"

Carrie looked thoughtfully at a dirty stuffed rabbit she had scavenged from under her bed. "Maybe you'll get to see Carrot Top?"

After helping Carrie clean up for a couple hours (and being delightfully rewarded with fresh oatmeal cookies afterward), I decided to head back home. I took the longest route back, using small side streets and even riding along the beach. But after a while it started to get dark and I didn't want to incur my mom's wrath. The last time I got home after dark on my bike she was in tears with a phone clutched in her hand, ready to call the local hospitals.

I stuck my bike in the garage, looking sadly at the discarded holiday lights piled on the floor on my way into the house.

"Oh, look who's home after pouting," my mother announced. "Have you recovered from your little tantrum?" She was wearing rubber gloves and scrubbing the kitchen sink, blasting some weird opera music.

I didn't dignify her with a response and instead skulked by and went to my room, giving my door a "light" slam. Before I could even settle down in front of my laptop to complain about my horrendous holiday plans on the Internet, the door flew open. My mother stood in the doorway, rubber gloves–clad hands on her hips.

"Mooooom, can you KNOCK?"

"Yeah, yeah. What are you doing in here that's so *private* anyway? Nothing, I'm sure, ha!" I couldn't tell if she really thought she was making a joke or if she was just determined to send me over the edge today.

I glared at her from my desk chair. "Ha. Ha. Can I *help* you?"

"Yes, you can help by being a good daughter for once and say, 'Why, thank you, Mother, for planning such a fun vacation! So many poor children in the world never go on vacation! I am SO grateful.'"

I could literally taste the barf rising in my throat. "Most poor children are lucky they don't have to go to Las Vegas."

There was a half second when I thought my mom might laugh, but instead she pointed a hot-pink-gloved finger at me and said, "You are going to get over this bad mood and have fun on this trip. Actually, I don't care if you have fun. Just be quiet and don't ruin the trip for everyone else! OTHER people's kids are happy to be going!"

And with that, she walked out, leaving my door wide open. My dad popped his head in. "Hey, Holly, you want curry for dinner?"

My head was starting to hurt. "I don't care, whatever."

"You don't CARE? Okay, maybe I'll ask my other daughter who cares when her father cooks for her!" He amiably walked toward Ann's room.

My family made me feel like the biggest ingrate on the planet.

THIRTEEN

. . . .

POOR FOLK: GET CREATIVE
THIS HOLIDAY SEASON!

Hoisting my Santa Claus bag of goodies over my shoulder, I walked toward the usual lunch spot in the Quad. I spotted Liz first — you couldn't miss her multiple shopping bags and Santa hat. Only Liz could manage to make holiday costume wear fashionable.

She greeted me with a hug and a "Merry almost-Christmas!" She also handed me a sparkly holiday gift bag filled to the brim with wrapped objects.

"LIZ! This is way too much stuff! As usual!"

"Oh, whatever. Like I have a budget," she said, waving her hand dismissively. I couldn't argue with that. I handed her my gift, which was wrapped in newspaper comics and fat pastel yarn. Only the very best for my friends.

"Ooooh!" She accepted it gleefully. Liz loves receiving gifts — one of the reasons I love her so much. I mean, she literally could buy herself whatever she wanted. She even liked that hideous bobcat statue I made in my ceramics class and gave her that one year. That's a true friend.

Eventually Carrie and David met up with us, also armed with gifts. It was time for our annual last-day-of-school-before-the-holiday-break gift exchange. We looked forward to this every year — almost as much as the MTV Video Music Awards, when we sat around Liz's huge flat screen and made fun of everyone's outfits.

Carrie gleefully collected her gifts and growled, "MINE!" David tried to snatch a couple away from her, resulting in Carrie rolling around in the dirt trying to keep them out of his reach. I swear, Carrie's the brother David never had.

"Oh my Lord, can you guys behave?" Liz cried, trying not to laugh. Soon we sat around in a circle with our presents piled up in front of us.

"Me first!" I exclaimed. I picked up Carrie's, a box wrapped in brown butcher paper and green-and-red bamboo-fiber ribbon, and shook it next to my ear.

"Oh, please, like that ever works," Carrie scoffed.

I carefully opened it, peeling the paper back meticulously so that it didn't rip. Carrie groaned in frustration. "HOLLY! You're killing me. Get on with it!"

"Okay, okay, sheesh!"

I squealed when I saw it was a DVD set of the entire British *Office* series. "Awesome! Yes, yes, yes!"

"It has a bunch of extra commentary from Ricky Gervais," Carrie said excitedly while I read the description on the back cover. "We need to revisit the entire series!" All of us had spent the previous summer completely obsessed with the show. Well, except Liz, who said she couldn't stand all the British mumbling. "WHAT are they saying?" she'd yell before storming out of the room.

We all opened the rest of our gifts — I got a ton of great books from both David and Liz, including a first edition copy of *A Tree Grows in Brooklyn*. Liz got me an array of nail polishes in hopes of me actually wearing some. Hehe, good luck.

I excitedly watched everyone open my gifts. I had made them mixed CDs with hand-drawn cover "art," and little photo albums that held a bunch of our pictures from the past few years.

"Awesome!" Carrie exclaimed as she flipped through the album.

David laughed and pointed to his CD. "I see the first track is an RMD classic." (I had included my favorite Raw Meat Demons song — "Headbutt into My Soul.")

"Oh my God, I almost forgot about these Halloween costumes!" Liz pointed at a photo of her, Carrie, and me dressed up as zombie Jonas Brothers. We snickered over the bloody brains splattered on Carrie's face. "So when are you leaving for the city of dreams?" she asked while tidily putting away her wrapping paper in small folded piles.

"Tomorrow morning," I groaned. "We're driving, of course."

David shook his head. "That sucks, man. But you get to just chill with your cousins and eat a lot, right?"

"I guess. I love my cousins. But even they can't make up for Vegas."

Carrie twirled a long strand of hair around her finger and frowned. "Well, at least you'll probably see a Christmas tree or two there. My parents have banned Christmas trees."

"WHY?" I asked incredulously.

"Um, because it's killing trees. Duh."

David snorted. "Do they not use paper, then?"

"Recycled only," Carrie said with a sigh.

Liz shook her head. "Your parents would die if they saw our house. I think we have five Christmas trees. They were shipped in the other day."

My jaw dropped. "Shipped in? By who? Your Christmas servants? Also, you guys aren't even going to be around on Christmas! Aren't you going skiing in Big Bear?"

"Yes, we are. But my parents like to embrace these American traditions wholeheartedly. Plus, they want to make sure our neighbors don't think we're terrorists."

David laughed. "That explains why your parents have like, five American flags in your front yard."

I looked at him. "So, what awesome plans do you have this Christmas? Family skateboarding?"

He shrugged. "You know. The usual. Driving out to Phoenix to hang with my grandparents. Excitement abounds.

Maybe this year my grandpa will actually stay awake through Christmas dinner."

The lunch bell rang and we scattered off to class. I said good-bye reluctantly — it was the first time I was ever sad to be leaving school for vacation.

FOURTEEN

. . . .

HOLIDAY HORROR: TEEN BLUDGEONS ENTIRE FAMILY TO DEATH WITH IPOD

I grasped for the car handle and stumbled my way out of the giant black Expedition. My knees were weak when my feet touched the ground, and I almost wanted to kneel before the Caesars Palace Hotel and kiss the scorching brick-paved ground. I had just spent six hours in an SUV packed with seven cousins watching WALL•E three times on the DVD system, trying to hold down my lunch. Did I mention that I sometimes get severely carsick, even on five-minute trips to the grocery store?

I looked up at the spectacle before me. There it was. In broad daylight, the neon lights and garish glitter of all that was horribly wrong with America: Las Vegas.

The sky was the color of dirty old blue jeans. Everywhere

I looked, giant buildings loomed above us, but not in the compact way of most cities. Instead the awkwardly massive hotels and their various attractions were spread out like one big strip mall.

I had to squint against the sun's glare because of all the mirrored walls and shiny glass. What is WITH Vegas and making things so shiny? It doesn't matter, though, because everything still looks and feels dirty.

For example, everywhere we walked on the strip, there were men slapping these plastic fliers for strippers in our faces, their sad-sack kids sitting on the sidewalk ledge behind them. I saw a man in an Elvis costume posing halfheartedly for pictures with gleeful Japanese tourists while simultaneously trying to sell some kind of car parked behind him.

This was where hundreds of families wanted to spend Christmas? I just didn't get it.

A total of four SUVs had been commissioned to haul all thirty of us from various locations in Southern California. Needless to say, no family member of mine (or family friend, for that matter) would be caught dead on a plane to Las Vegas. Why make a quick and comfortable journey when you could sniff seven other people's body odor for six hours? The immigrant experience is a rich one.

After we all checked into our rooms, Ann and I decided to do some exploring, letting our parents know that we would meet up with them in a couple hours. In the chaos of getting everyone situated, my parents absentmindedly nodded their permission. We made our way through the hotel, eventually walking into Caesars Palace's sprawling mall, the Forum.

The ceilings were painted to look like the sky, pale blue with puffy angelic clouds. I think it was supposed to feel like we were outside because I noticed that the sky gradually changed colors as if the sun was setting and rising.

I elbowed Ann and pointed. "Who are they kidding? This is so sad."

Ann looked up and shrugged. "I think it looks kind of pretty."

I stared at her openmouthed, then shook my head. "Have you learned nothing from being my sister?" Ann rolled her eyes and walked ahead of me.

We eventually approached a replica of Michelangelo's statue of David in all its naked glory and immediately started cracking up. Someone had perched a giant Santa hat on his head. And did I mention he was naked?

"Where are we having dinner?" Ann asked as we walked across a three-foot-long wood "bridge" over a mini-canal running neon-blue water by the Versace store.

"At the buffet. Where else?"

I love to eat. And normally, I am all for buffets. But a Vegas buffet was on a whole other level. It felt too gluttonous, even for the holidays. Have you ever seen how many leftovers are carted off by the busboys? It literally makes me think of starving children. If starving children knew what the hell to do with five thousand crab legs as big as their own legs.

Ann pulled out her camera while we were in the Forum. She's really gotten into photography, so she was lugging around this fancy digital one that my parents got her for her birthday, taking pictures of this and that. We took particular pleasure in a shot of me picking my nose in front of the Prada store. We took off running when we saw a saleslady (wearing what looked like a fancy black straightjacket) rush to the window.

I quickly grew bored, however, because really how many "sunsets" and "rainstorms" can one take while walking past the Gap? It was almost dinnertime anyway, so we headed back to our hotel room to meet up with everyone. It was quite a trek.

Huffing and puffing in the elevator, Ann moaned, "Why did it take us fifteen minutes to walk from the lobby to the elevator?"

"I know. Everything in this place is gigantic. Like, I think they base the architecture on how much dumb, tacky stuff they can cram in here," I grumbled while pushing the button for the nineteenth floor.

Ann threw me an exasperated look. "Yeah, yeah, you hate Las Vegas. We get it."

The elevator doors opened before I could think of a good comeback, and we were face-to-face with twenty-eight family members crammed into the elevator lobby. Everyone began talking at once, yelling at us for disappearing. Ann decided to head out with them for dinner, while I told them I'd meet up after I showered.

I waved good-bye to the herd and fled to my hotel room — relieved to be rid of everyone, even just temporarily. The only good thing about being on vacation with so many people was that you could slip out fairly unnoticed. Even my mom's hawk eye took a break when she was in vacation mode.

As I showered in a bathroom bigger than my living room back home, I thought about the days ahead and wanted to bury myself in the fluffy white hotel blankets. Christmas was still three days away, and I was already sick of this place.

FIFTEEN

. . . .

CHRISTMAS EVE DRAMA UNFOLDS AT CAESARS PALACE; GAMBLING STILL HAPPENING, THOUGH

By the time Christmas Eve rolled around, I was so over it. Most of all, I was tired of how annoyingly chapped my lips got from the recirculated air in our hotel room. My lips would like to say a big F YOU, Caesars Palace.

My parents, along with the other adults, were unusually giddy with excitement — they almost let us kids do whatever the heck we wanted. "Merry Christmas Eve, girls!" my mom practically sang as she busted into our hotel suite that morning. My sister and I grunted from where we were lying side by side on our shared bed, watching *Storage Wars* on TV. We were still in our pajamas while some of our cousins had already gone downstairs for the breakfast buffet. "You're not going to stay inside all day, are you?" she demanded as she yanked open the curtains that were heavy enough to shield the entire hotel from an air raid. Ann and I hissed like vampires as the sun touched our faces.

"Mooom! It's too bright!" Ann whined, shielding herself with her arm.

Normally, this sort of lazy bratfest would have had my mom on our asses so quick we'd be downstairs and dressed in record time. But this was Happy Vegas Mom.

"It's a beautiful day! Guess what you guys get to do on Christmas Eve?"

We stared at her in silence.

"You get to go SHOPPING! For your own gifts!"

Ann finally showed a sign of life. "Really?!" she asked, sitting straight up for the first time all morning.

"Yes! This way, you get exactly what you want! Isn't that fun?"

"We have to BUY our own presents?" I asked. I knew that I sounded like a giant spoiled baby. But I didn't want to choose my own gift. That was NOT Christmasy.

My mom looked crestfallen. "What's the problem now? I thought you girls would love this! You never like the stuff I pick out anyway!"

It was true. Every year my mom bought us stuff like matching sweater sets, or gift cards to movie theatres or Starbucks. Honestly, she was the queen of regifting things her coworkers had gotten her, like the time we got Crabtree & Evelyn lotion that made us smell like old ladies. But at least she thought of us for a nanosecond, and then gift wrapped something. This was just depressing.

"I just . . . it's not right!" I exclaimed. And to my surprise, tears started pricking my eyes.

My mom stared at me, aghast. "I can't do anything right!" Then she shook her head and left the room, calling out, "Do whatever you want. The cash is on the table. Meet us for dinner at the buffet at six."

When she was gone, Ann gave me a weird look. "What's your problem? Are you on your period or something?" I threw a pillow at her face, which made her scream and then storm into the bathroom, slamming the heavy double doors behind her.

Ah, the beauty of Christmas.

I sulked in my bed, flipping channels until it landed on *Home Alone*. Oh, geez. Yet I couldn't stop watching because everything about the movie looked so darn Christmasy and cozy that I was able to transport myself out of this place.

Ann eventually came out of the bathroom, fully dressed and ready for the day. "BYE-BYE, CRAZY!" she hollered before leaving the room with another loud slam. Damn, those doors were *heavy*.

I refused to leave my bed and finished watching *Home Alone*. Around three o'clock my dad came into the room. "STILL sleeping?!" he asked incredulously.

"Noooo, I'm watching classic American cinema, can't you see?" I said.

"Okay, well, the uncles are going golfing. I think your mom and the aunts are shopping."

"Wow. You guys have really changed up your extracurricular activities on vacation."

My dad just looked at me, probably wondering how to communicate with this alien creature in front of him. He eventually shrugged and said, "Suit yourself, as always. Don't forget to eat!" He pulled a couple boxes of cookies and crackers and a banana from a shopping bag he was carrying and left them on the table before walking out. I looked at the snacks with guilt. And then ate them because I was starving.

I picked up the remote and changed the channel again. "Ooh, a *Downton Abbey* marathon!" I exclaimed to myself, submerging deeper into the blankets. I wondered if this was the first time in history that someone in a Vegas hotel room was watching an English countryside drama. I didn't realize I had dozed off until the bleep of my cell phone woke me up.

WHEARE YOU?

I blinked and read it again.

WHEARE YOU?

My mom was the worst texter ever.

I looked at the time. "Oh, crap." It was 6:06, and I was late for dinner. I typed "On my way" and got up with a lazy stretch. I threw on a pair of skinny jeans without holes in them and a loose tank with a long gray cardigan, and stepped into my black combat boots. This was dressy for me — I hoped it was appreciated. I put on a neon-pink braided bracelet from Liz for a festive touch and ran out the door.

When the elevator reached the lobby, I squeezed myself between an old woman and a little boy and headed toward the casino. I took a moment to survey the scene before me. Slot machines were noisily going off at every turn, and everyone seemed to be drunk already. A large group of girls wearing tiaras and beauty pageant sashes stumbled by in mile-high heels. Wow, when did bachelorette parties become bigger skankfests than Halloween? Behind them, ironically, was a wedding party. Wow, a winter wonderland wedding in Vegas. So jealous.

I stood in the casino for a minute, reading all the signs and "roadmaps," looking for the buffet. What was WITH these hotels? It was like navigating through a city designed by a really excited four-year-old. WHAT DOES IT MEAN WHEN AN ARROW POINTS DOWN? Where in God's name is that pointing to???

Before I could smash the signs to bits with my bare hands, I felt a slight bump against my right leg and looked down.

It was the little boy from the elevator. He was smiling toothily up at me. I smiled back politely and continued to study the maps. Two seconds later, I felt someone tug on the bottom of my sweater.

"What the — ?!" It was the little boy again. He clutched a beanbag replica of a Coca-Cola bottle and repeatedly poked me in the thigh with it. I was looking around for his parents when he poked me extra hard in the knee.

"Ow! You little twerp!" I stared down at him again. He seemed about three years old, and was wearing a neon-green nylon backpack with a matching neon-green nylon cap, a sweatshirt that said LAS VEGAS! on it, and tiny khaki shorts. I felt a sympathetic pang of understanding. Poor little Asian dude.

I tried to escape by walking extra fast in between the "Roman" pillars and slot machines. I glanced behind me and was relieved to see that he was nowhere in sight. I tried to reorient myself, looking for more signs.

I almost jumped a mile when I felt a familiar poke in my leg. The boy had magically reappeared by my side.

"How in the world?! Where are your parents, kid?" There was a sea of Asians walking throughout the casino and sitting down at slot machines and blackjack tables. They could be anywhere.

I knelt before him and asked in slow English, "Where. Are. Your. PARENTS? Mommy, Daddy?"

He just smiled, poked me in the nose with his Coca-Cola toy, and ran off.

"Crap! Come back here!" I chased after him, keeping my eye on the darting neon-green spot ahead of me. He was fast, and I had to sprint to keep up with him. When he bumped into people, his little neon hat momentarily came to a halt, and then he quickly darted around them.

I had finally gotten to about two feet behind him, where he was standing next to a couple sitting down at a slot machine called Nickel Heaven!!!, when someone tapped me on the shoulder. I spun around to see an elderly man in a Caesars Palace polo shirt looking at me sternly. He was a good three inches shorter than me and had a giant white mustache, looking like Mario and Luigi's grandfather.

"You're not allowed in the casino, young lady."

At first I got scared of being "in trouble," but then a flash of irritation whipped through me. "I know, I'm just trying to find this kid —"

"I don't care what you're *doing*. There is a strict policy of no minors on the casino floor."

"Can you just listen to me for a second? I'm not *gambling*. I mean, how many fifteen-year-olds come here and go buck wild on the slot machines? I just —"

"That's it! I'm walkin' you out!" he said with his hands on his hips.

"Excuse me? Walk me out to where? I have to meet my family for dinner at the buffet. And I just lost this little kid who is roaming around alone!"

Then, amazingly, the old dude had the nerve to push me from behind, toward the row of doors leading out of the casino and onto the strip. Grandpa was pretty damn strong. I slid across the burgundy-and-gold carpets, bumping into the glass doors at the very end. "HEY! I have to meet my family for dinner! I'm a guest at this hotel!" I started yelling, hoping to attract enough attention to flee this Casino Nazi. Unfortunately, everybody seemed way too busy to notice. What *happens* to people when they come here?!

I was ceremoniously dumped outside with a final stern look from the "security guard," who I could have sworn dusted off his hands like a Warner Brothers cartoon character. "Learn to listen to your elders, young lady!"

Before the shock of what just happened could wear off, I spotted a neon-green flash in the reflection of the glass double doors. I spun around to see the twerp right in front of me, in runner's position. He waved at me and started off down the Vegas strip, dodging a few cars in the hotel's massive driveway.

Ugh ugh ugh! I wanted to kill this little kid. As I crossed an intersection, a huge Escalade honked at me and something in me snapped. I flipped it off as I sprinted away. Don't even. With my eyes focused on the neon dot of the kid's hat, I ran by groups of people drinking out of huge margarita cups the length of broomsticks. Seriously? I mean, you need to drink *that* badly? To the point where you must keep a barrel's worth of alcohol in a bright-red never-ending tube with you at *all times*? Also, it was so hot, it felt like a blow-dryer was blasting me in the face. I had heard how the desert could be freezing in the winter, but of course Vegas had been unseasonably warm since we got here. HURRAY.

Bitter thoughts continued to pulse through me as I jogged down the strip. I lost sight of the kid and stopped in front of the New York–New York hotel. The roller coaster in front zoomed by, and I heard the fleeting joyful screams of its passengers.

I glared at it. Was everyone *really* having that good of a time here? Was there something wrong with them, or something wrong with me?

That's when I noticed the kid. He was across the street, heading back toward our hotel. GAH!

I sprinted off again, almost running over entire families and couples holding hands. I had reached the Bellagio when I noticed that everyone was strangely hushed and the air felt thick and still. I slowed down to see what all the fuss was about, when I saw him again. He was leaning against the railing between two large tourists, his little feet on tippy toes and his cap pushed back off his forehead. I shoved my way up to him and tapped his backpack, my mouth open, ready to start scolding.

But before I could say anything, he grabbed my arm, pointed at the still "lagoon" in front of us, and said, "Look!"

A swell of soft violins and trembling cellos filled the hot night. The music was quiet at first, slowly growing louder and more dramatic. I looked around, confused. Was this some sort of concert? But then I realized there was no band — the music was being piped in through stereos hidden around the front of the ornately manicured garden.

The still, dark water in front of us turned shades of deep purples and greens, and arcs of water shot across each other. I hoisted my body over the railing to get a better look. The lights and streams of water followed every dip and peak of the music perfectly. They were synchronized, like dancers, and I couldn't look away. A cheesy opera song was playing, but it sounded beautiful and strangely poetic. The lights glowed in every color and the music vibrated through the ground, into my toes, and into the railing I was holding on to. A spray of water hit my face and

I felt truly cooled down for the first time since I arrived in Vegas.

I looked at the kid, who was completely entranced by the water show. Everyone near us had the same awestruck expressions on their faces. Some were pointing at things, oohing and aahing, while others were taking photos and videos with their cell phones.

When the music faded out and the water grew still again, everyone started clapping and cheering. And then a weird thing happened. Suddenly all the immigrant families around me weren't embarrassing. They weren't misguided. They weren't pathetic.

They were just happy.

Not only did the kid speak English, he wouldn't shut up. The entire walk back to the hotel, he talked nonstop — about his turtle, his teacher, his shoes, his backyard, his favorite dinosaur, and his favorite water show — the Bellagio's.

"And sometimes, it plays Fank Sonata instead of the orchestra. Because then the water is fast."

"Uh-huh, that's cool. We have to find your parents now. They're probably very worried about you," I told him as we walked back into Caesars Palace. As soon as we were in the lobby, I saw a huge group of people in a panic.

Oh crap.

A teenage girl yelled out, "Benny!" All the heads swiveled and a stampede of feet rushed toward us. A woman who was in tears swooped him up and started half-yelling/half-talking to him rapidly in Chinese. There were several

Caesars Palace workers nearby, looking relieved. One of them was that geezer who had thrown me out. I made a face at him, and he looked away hastily.

"Benny! Where were you! Thank God, oh thank God!" the woman clutching him kept saying over and over again. I assumed she was his mom.

Benny pointed at me. "I was with her! Her name is Holly!"

His mother looked up at me, wiping her face. "Who are you?"

I rushed to explain so that they wouldn't think I was some teenage kidnapper weirdo. "I saw him run out of the hotel alone, so I chased after him. He's okay!"

Benny's mom gripped my arm with both her hands. "I can't thank you enough! His grandmother has been feeling so guilty!" The old woman from the elevator was lying down on a lobby sofa, with relatives hovering over her.

"I'm sorry," I said instinctively.

She waved her hand dismissively. "No, no, we are so grateful!"

I was getting really embarrassed and starting to mumble something unintelligible when I heard someone yell my name.

It was my mom, running across the lobby. "Holly! Where have you been?" She was all disheveled and out of breath. Oops.

"Sorry, Mom. First I got lost, and then I found this kid, and then he ran away, and then I had to get him, and now —"

"I called and called you! What's wrong with you?! Why didn't you answer your phone? Do you know how worried we've all been?" Her voice had reached epic angry-mom mode, and everyone was staring.

"I know, I'm sorry! The thing is —"

"You *always* have some excuse. Always, always! You've ruined this trip from the first day! Are you *happy* now?" I honestly thought my mom was going to start crying. I was speechless.

"Excuse me," Benny's mom said. "I think maybe there is a misunderstanding. Please be kind to your daughter. She was helping us — she found my son who got lost!"

My mom looked startled. "What?"

I totally got uncomfortable, just like I always did when people said nice things about me in front of a lot of people. I tried to steer my mom away. "Okay, let's go."

Benny's mother continued talking, though. "Our son, Benny, left the hotel and she ran after him. If she didn't do that, who knows what could have happened!"

My mom looked at me. "Is this true?"

"Uh, yes."

"That's why you were late? Why didn't you just say so?" she asked, throwing up her arms.

"I was trying to but you didn't give me a chance!"

She turned red as she looked around at Benny's family, who were all watching us curiously. The one person who hated making a spectacle in public more than me was my mother.

"You are very lucky to have such a good daughter like her," Benny's mom said with a wink.

I almost died.

My mom regarded me for a second. "Yes, I suppose I am."

"Okaaay. Come on, let's go, I'm starving," I said, tugging on my mom's arm.

I felt a tug on my own arm, and saw Benny waving good-bye to me with his Coca-Cola bottle. I smiled and gave him a little hug, then hurriedly waved good-bye to everyone else. His mother embraced me in a huge, embarrassing hug.

"Are you okay, then?" my mom asked as we walked to the buffet.

"Yes, of course, I'm fine!"

"Well, just . . . don't disappear like that again. I don't care how old you are, a parent is always going to worry about their child. Especially one who doesn't have a good sense of direction."

Ah, and there it was. Can't be too mushy in the Kim household.

At one point I looked back and saw Benny's family walking toward the casino. They were all wearing variations of denim shorts and khakis with Las Vegas sweatshirts, surrounded by gold mirrors and jewel tones, women in skintight dresses, and old men in baseball caps.

And you know what? It really looked like Christmas.

BHS HOLIDAY SURVEY
HOW DID YOU CELEBRATE THE HOLIDAYS?

My family and I went to Aspen, and then my brother Joey broke his ribs. My parents got really pissed and we had to have Christmas dinner in the hospital cafeteria.

— HEATHER A., FRESHMAN

My grandparents came over and I had to eat fruitcake, which I fed to the cat. And then he threw up. The end.

— MARK R., SENIOR

We went to Paris. I got Chanel sunglasses.

— LAUREN P., JUNIOR

I went to Las Vegas and rescued a child. It was okay.

— HOLLY K., SOPHOMORE

FEBRUARY

Dear Loving Classmates,

Okay, who is it? I'm serious, if this is a joke I will hunt you down and torture you with my bare hands. And maybe some rusty tools.

What am I referring to, you ask? Oh, just the "mysterious" cliché notes and crap everywhere I go. This has to be a joke — I mean, who in the world likes me that much? Making a mockery of me? *That* I understand. Irritation and exasperation are sentiments that are shot my way daily, and I've become totally accustomed to them by now. If this isn't a joke, I apologize for making fun of your adolescent longings, but enough is enough. Valentine's Day is slowly approaching, and it's freaking me out.

Everyone hates on Valentine's Day, and I am the Queen Hatemonger of this day. Not only is it completely superficial and torturous for single people everywhere, I just find it so embarrassing. Flowers and declarations of love? WE'RE IN HIGH SCHOOL. Nobody really cares about anybody that much — it's impossible. Our self-absorbed, pimply heads can't really feel that strongly for anyone other than ourselves.

It's sad but true, and it's about time some-body admitted it. And reading crap like *Romeo and Juliet* only reinforces these myths about teenage love. So does every episode of *The Vampire Diaries*, *90210*, and every other television show that pretends that teenagers have any notions of love.

So as everyone gets all hormonal and pres-sured to swap ridiculous Hallmark cards and find someone to take to another lame dance, I'll be sitting here, counting the hours until this charade is over and we can move on to St. Patrick's Day.

Wearing green? Now that's a holiday I can support.

Barf and kisses,

Holly

SIXTEEN

. . . .

MYSTERIOUS AND GROTESQUE
HEART-SHAPED NOTES INFEST BAY HIGH

The secret admirer farce began with a heart-shaped Post-it note. It was hot pink and stuck to the outside of my locker like a shining beacon of embarrassment. Carrie snatched it off before I could read what was on it.

"Dear Holly of my heart — WHAT?!" She burst out laughing before she could finish reading.

I swung my backpack really hard against her arm before grabbing it out of her hands. What the heck was this?!

DEAR HOLLY OF MY HEART,
YOUR WORDS TOUCH ME LIKE THE SIGHT
OF CHERRY BLOSSOMS ON A RAINY
DAY. I HOPE TO TELL YOU ALL
ABOUT IT ONE DAY — IF I DARE.
LOVE,
    YOUR SECRET
    ADMIRER

Carrie peered over my shoulder and finished reading the message. She stared at me for a second before cracking up again. "Holy crap! Someone loves you! PUAHahahahah!"

I elbowed her and darted my eyes around to see if anyone had heard. "Shut up! No one loves me! This has to be a joke. It's probably D."

"What's probably D?" David asked as he rode up on his skateboard, gently nudging the row of lockers with the tip of his board as he came to a stop.

"Nothing. What's up?" I answered before Carrie could open her mouth. I shoved the Post-it into my jacket pocket and looked at David innocently. He regarded both of us suspiciously, and then shrugged. "Nothing. Do you guys wanna head over to PB to grab some burritos?"

"Yeah, let me get some things from my locker first." I opened my locker so that David's face was hidden behind it and mouthed, "Don't say anything," to Carrie before I shut it. I looked at the Post-it again and felt a weird somersault in my belly.

The sun reflected off the tiny mosaic tiles on our table at the Burrito Shack, and I brushed some crumbs off of it while thinking about the note. Who in the world would do such a thing? First, as a joke it was so not funny. Second, if it was serious, how dare they embarrass me and place it on the OUTSIDE of my locker for everyone to see? Also, nice freaking use of cheesy similes. Cherry blossoms? Was that some sort of reference to the Orient?

David let out a loud burp and both Carrie and Liz glared at him from across the table.

"GOD, David. So disgusting," Liz said, practically gagging.

"I'm going to barf up my burrito," Carrie said, staring at her bean and cheese sullenly. David cackled and shoved more tortilla chips into his mouth.

I looked sideways and squinted at him. If I found out it was him, I'd kick him in the face.

Carrie caught me looking at him and raised her eyebrows. I pursed my lips and glared at her. She rolled her eyes.

Liz sighed and pushed her enormous sunglasses up on top of her head, strands of her wavy hair tucked behind her ears. "So. Valentine's Day is coming up."

Carrie choked on her horchata. I ignored her and said, "Yeah, so?"

Liz propped her elbows on the table and stared out at the ocean morosely. "So, I don't have a Valentine, as usual. It's so depressing."

David pretended to snore and Liz shot him a dirty look. "It is! I'm probably going to end up hanging out with like, you guys that night. No offense."

"None taken!" Carrie said cheerfully, picking at a stain on her vintage camp sweatshirt. "Anyway, it's your own fault you don't have a Valentine. Every year like fifty guys ask you out and you reject them."

"Yeah! Steve literally, *literally* asks me about you every day. 'She's still not seeing anyone, right?'" David said with a sad shake of his moppy head. Steve was David's closest thing to a bro best friend. He also happened to be 5'2" and allergic to everything on Planet Earth. Guy never had a chance.

"Can't you just tell him I have a boyfriend?" Liz asked with exasperation.

David leaned back and stretched out his long legs. "Uh, no. I'm not doing any dirty work for you. And plus, you don't have a boyfriend? So that would be LYING."

"Give me a break. That would be better than dangling the poor guy around forever," I said.

"Who's dangling?!" Liz cried. "I never let him think he had an iota of a chance with me! Excuse me for having a heart and not saying, 'Sorry, Shrimptown, but never in your wildest dreams would I date you.'"

"That's true. But now all your niceness has Steve's hopes up," Carrie said.

"Ugh! Why don't any AWESOME guys ever like me?" Liz moaned.

I looked at her. "Are you seriously complaining about too many guys liking you right now?"

"Oh, please. Like you'd date the string of eligible bachelors that I have to deal with?" she asked, lifting an eyebrow.

"Do you know me? I don't 'date.'"

David laughed. "You still think boys have cooties."

Carrie tried to make meaningful eye contact with me again. "I do NOT. I just think that dating in high school is overrated. As if any of these relationships are going to last?" I asked with my eyebrows raised.

"Okay, I'm not looking for the love of my life or future husband, I just like the idea of having someone special on Valentine's Day."

I made a face. "Liz, seriously, who cares? You know Valentine's Day isn't even a real holiday, it's just something—"

"Yeah, yeah, 'made up by Hallmark to profit off the emotions of poor suckers who buy into it.' Well, whatever, I'm totally one of those suckers and I don't care. Why is finding a decent guy at BHS so impossible?!" Liz said, slamming her fist onto the table. Okaaay. Just a tad dramatic?

Carrie sighed. "I have the opposite problem. There are so many guys — and too little interest in me. So sad."

David got up. "All right, too much girl talk. I'm headed home. Catch ya later." He hopped onto his skateboard and sped off.

As soon as he was out of earshot, Carrie said, "Thank God! Holly — please can I tell Liz? Please please please?"

Liz looked at both of us blankly. "Tell me what?"

I groaned and waved my hand weakly in surrender. "Fine, whatever. I just don't want David to know — in case he's actually not trying to play some sick joke on me."

Carrie told Liz about the note excitedly and Liz squealed. "You have a secret admirer?!"

I shushed the two hyenas that I called my best friends. "No, I don't! I mean, it's totally a joke." I took the Post-it out of my pocket, uncrinkled it, and gave it to Liz. She held it close to her face and scrutinized it. Liz has a high threshold for cheesiness — she always cries during the "declarations of love" scenes in Julia Roberts movies (I may own *My Best Friend's Wedding*, but I do not cry!) — but even she started giggling when she read it.

"Cherry blossoms?!" she exclaimed.

"I know, right? Do you think that's some sort of crack about me being Asian? Like, comparing me to a delicate lotus blossom or something twisted like that?"

Liz threw me a weary look. "For God's sake, Holly, no. I just think he's trying to be poetic."

Carrie got a contemplative look on her face. "Do you really think it could be David?"

Liz's mouth dropped open. "Oh my God, you think David likes Holly?"

"Well . . . or he's playing a joke," Carrie replied thought-fully.

The thought of David loving me made me feel ill. It was like my brother being in love with me. So wrong.

"Well, I don't think this is a joke. I think someone really likes Holly," Liz said resolutely. What a surprise from Liz, the Valentine's Day sucker.

"That would be so awesome," Carrie said.

"Ew! No it would not. And if this person knew me at all, they'd know this kind of crap is not the way to my heart," I said grumpily, looking down at the offensive Post-it. It couldn't be for real, right?

SEVENTEEN

COLUMNIST HOLLY KIM VICTIM
OF DRIVE-BY VALENTINE

I stared at the computer screen, trying to think of another word for "stupid."

I was starting a new column, sitting in the journalism room with my brain at a total standstill. The March issue was coming up, and I was trying to consider what would be more worthwhile to complain about: popular kids with racist tendencies? Or something lighter, like people who post too many photos of their uncute dogs on Facebook?

Amir sat next to me and typed away. He had his headphones on and was rocking his head to the beat — undoubtedly some bad rap song about how awesome the rapper is at getting laid. He caught me staring at him and smiled widely before going back to his article.

A smile! What the heck was that? Was Amir, the über macho P90X fanatic, my secret admirer?

All day long, in each of my classes, I had been looking at every male classmate suspiciously. If they talked to me, they were immediately on my list of suspects because, quite frankly, few boys ever bothered speaking to me. I even looked at some of the girls apprehensively. Lesbians were also fair culprits — I'm sure some of them would find my assertive ways irresistible.

"Hey, Holly?" I looked away from Amir to see Isabel standing there with a funny look on her face.

"Yeah?"

She held out her hands and cradled gingerly in them was something very red, very heart-shaped, and very lacy. Oh, dear God.

"Um, this is for you," Isabel said with a big smile.

I grabbed it from her, feeling my face turn red. "Uh, thanks."

She waited for me to read it. I laughed nervously and asked, "Where did this come from?"

"It was really strange. I was sitting by the door, and I saw someone toss this into the class just now. He ran off and when I looked outside, he was gone," she said.

"He? Did you see who he was?!" I yelped.

"No, he ran off too fast. I don't even remember what he was wearing. Now that I think about it, I can't even be sure that it was a guy. . . ."

Yeah. Really helpful. What in the world? I was trying to digest this information when I noticed that Isabel was still standing there. I guess she wanted me to explain the heart.

"Okay, thanks!" I shoved the glaring-red obstruction into my backpack and turned back to the computer screen purposefully. She stood there for a few more seconds before walking off. For the rest of the hour, I caught her looking at me out of the corner of her eye every so often. I feigned obliviousness.

As soon as the bell rang for lunch, I hit "save," grabbed my backpack, and ran to the nearest girls' bathroom. I rushed into a stall and slammed the door shut, making sure to lock it about ten times. My heart beat fast as I held the valentine in my hands.

It was a huge construction-paper heart that opened up into a card, with lace glued all around the edges and "Holly" printed in a script font on the cover. It was all very elaborate.

I opened up the card, and sequined metallic hearts fell out. Geez. This is what was inside:

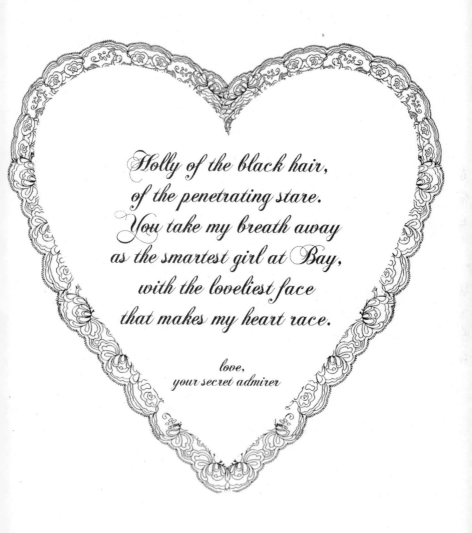

Holly of the black hair,
of the penetrating stare.
You take my breath away
as the smartest girl at Bay,
with the loveliest face
that makes my heart race.

love,
your secret admirer

My cheeks started to burn intensely, and I got a funny feeling in my stomach. I probably sat on the toilet seat for about an hour staring at that card. It was so cheesy, but . . . it was kind of well written. And kind of, well, nice.

Gah! What was I thinking? I was not taking this secret admirer seriously, was I?

I walked out into the Quad to meet everyone for lunch — the valentine burning a hole in my backpack. I was so out of it that I bumped right into Matthew. Matthew F-ing Reynolds.

"Heeey, Holly K.," he said with a quick flash of his ridiculous heartthrob smile.

I smiled instinctively. "Hi! Hi, Matthew! What's up?!" Okay, did those words just come out of my mouth in that high-pitched voice? Kill me! This day was just getting worse and worse.

He nodded slowly and said, "Nothin' much. What are you up to these days?"

Before I could answer some guy ran into him in a fake tackle. They both started cracking up, leaving me to stand there awkwardly. I mean, was I supposed to answer him? Or was it just like, a courtesy "How are you?" I seriously stood there contemplating this until I realized that both of them had already run off laughing.

Sigh.

Having this teeny tiny crush on Matthew was turning me into a loser out of a bad teen movie from the '90s.

Just then I had a flash of hope. Could Matthew be . . . ?

Don't worry. I only thought that for another two seconds

before the normal Holly pointed to sad-sap Holly and laughed. *"Are you insane?!"* I quickly dashed those thoughts away and ran off to find my friends.

Liz arrived at my house around four o'clock, breathless and looking about as disheveled as she could ever look. Two strands of hair were out of place.

"Well?! Show it to me!" she demanded after running up the stairs and into my bedroom. I shushed her, scrambling to usher her in and shut the door. She kicked off her suede ankle boots and plopped onto my bed.

"Shh! I don't want Ann snooping around — she'd ruin my life. Here it is!" I shoved the valentine into her hands. While Liz sat on my gray-and-white striped bedspread and ravenously read the poem, I bit the inside of my cheeks, waiting for her reaction. I had decided to show Liz, not Carrie, this particular valentine. I don't know, I just didn't feel like having Carrie make fun of it. For some reason I now felt weirdly protective of my "secret admirer." Not that I liked it/him or anything.

Liz looked up at me with this bizarre gaping expression on her face.

"What?" I asked defensively.

She dramatically fell backward onto my bed and held the valentine up to her heart. "This is the most romantic thing I've ever read."

I felt my face get hot again, and I paced around my room, fiddling with various objects to avoid looking at her. "Liz! Don't be crazy. I just need to find out who it is," I said while tinkering with a metal robot toy that David had won for me at a carnival last year.

"Well, whoever he is, he has to be . . . sensitive. And hopefully really hot," Liz added. She sat in a puddle of her pale-pink pleated skirt, a dreamy expression on her face.

"Yeah. I'm sure a really hot guy feels that way about me. If anything, it's probably one of the geeks who hang out by my locker."

And then, I had a revelation.

I always made fun of these four guys who hung out by my locker. You know the type: They spend their nights playing online first-person shooter games, devote their lunches to quibbling about the merits of the old *Star Wars* films versus the new ones, and probably have never spoken to a girl in their lives. Geek-o-rama.

And the reason they always hung out by my locker was because one of them, Daniel Milford, had a locker right next to mine. I had always suspected that he had a little crush on me because of an incident in third grade.

We had been assigned a family tree project, and Daniel and I sat at the same table. There was a big pile of crayons spread out in the middle of the table and as I meticulously shaded in my variegated green leaves, I noticed that Daniel's leaves were purple. His head was bent over his work, his tongue sticking out a little in concentration.

I also noticed that Cindy Masters was watching him and giggling. I stared at Daniel's leaves for a second. "Why are you coloring your tree purple? Trees aren't purple."

He looked up at me, then at Cindy, then at his tree. He slowly unclenched his fist around the purple crayon and placed it back in the pile. He stared at the crayons — fingers twitching over them, not sure of which one to pick up.

"You *are* colorblind!" Cindy squealed with glee.

Daniel turned bright red and flipped his paper over. I glared at Cindy and said, "Did you tell him that the purple crayon was green?"

She rolled her eyes and gave me a bitchy little look. "So what? It's funny. He can't even tell the difference."

I don't know what came over me at that moment, but looking at Daniel's sad purple tree and still hands shot a surge of pure rage through me that at the tender age of eight, I had never felt before. I grabbed all the purple crayons from the pile, all six of them, and before Cindy knew what was happening I threw them — really hard — at her face.

Ever since that day, Daniel Milford had been silently protective over me. I can't explain it. It's not a daily event, more like an every-once-in-a-while general feeling: like when I realized he picked out the nicest math book to hand to me on the first day of school, or let me cut in front of him in the lunch line.

It was all so clear now. He was finally ready to make his true feelings known!

I must've had a strange look on my face, because Liz shot up and demanded, "What? Do you think you know who it is?"

"Yeah. I think it's Daniel."

She tilted her head, puzzled. "Who's that?"

"You know. Daniel Milford — his locker is right next to mine."

"What — you mean that geek who dressed up as a ninja robot for Halloween?!"

"Er . . . yeah. Him."

"What makes you think it's him? Did you see him put something in your locker?"

I fell back onto my bed next to her. "No. But I have my reasons."

Liz raised an immaculately plucked eyebrow. "Tell me!"

"Well, one time in elementary school —"

"ELEMENTARY SCHOOL?" Liz interrupted.

"Just shut it and let me finish! One time when we were in third grade I kind of stood up for him against this bitchy hag named Cindy Masters, and I think he's been like, carrying a torch for me all this time."

Liz stared at me in disbelief. "*This* is your hunch?"

"Yes! I think I'm right, too."

"I don't know. . . . I mean, what are the current signs? You can't trace this valentine back to one day in the third grade for Pete's sake."

I sat up abruptly. "Yes I can!"

Liz stretched out on the bed. "I think you'd better be pretty sure it's him. I still wonder about David, too."

Repulsed, I hit her arm. "Ew! This would be a joke way beyond even him!"

"But I mean, these valentines really border on the

cheesy. They could totally be a joke." I blinked a couple times and Liz quickly followed up with, "Not that you having a secret admirer would be a joke, of course! I'm just saying that D can be a tricky one."

A little injured, I said, "He would never do anything like this. It's too gross."

Liz looked at me skeptically. "Well, boys are known to be gross on occasion."

EIGHTEEN

VALENTINE DRIVE-BY SOLVED? OR ARE WE JUST DRAGGING THIS OUT LIKE THE MOVIE ENDING OF *LORD OF THE RINGS*?

Now that I was hell-bent on Daniel being my secret admirer, all signs pointed glaringly, neon-brightly, obviously to him.

The next morning at school, I casually hung around my locker a little longer than I needed to, pretending to rummage around for a book while I waited for Daniel to show up. When he did, I looked at him with new eyes. And it wasn't a pretty picture.

Daniel was one of those boys whose hair always looked dirty. Not cute-rock-boy dirty, but like, no-shower-because-I-am-yucky dirty. His hair was a little long and hung greasily in front of his eyes. It was also dyed black. (Daniel's a natural redhead.) Tall and awkward, he always looked like he was in danger of falling over. And he wore T-shirts with dragons printed on them. In other words: pure hotness.

He stopped in front of his locker and caught me staring at him. Uh-oh. Before I could react, he quickly averted his eyes and in the process dropped his backpack on the floor. This made him reach down quickly and knock into a girl on his left. She threw him a dirty look and said, "Watch it, dork." He turned bright red, mumbled an apology, and kind of ran off down the hallway.

Well.

I just stood there feeling pretty proud of myself. Daniel was totally my secret admirer — why else would he be so flustered? Now, the question was, how would I let him down? Valentine's Day was the next day and I had to stop things before he embarrassed himself. I mean, he's a nice guy and all, but really, Daniel Milford and me? I don't think so.

My opportunity came during fifth period: World History. Daniel was in my class, and I planned to drop some subtle hints his way.

Everyone was milling around and talking when I got to class. I looked at the clock. Five minutes. That would be plenty of time.

Daniel was sitting at his desk, playing some game on his cell phone. Without being too creepy, I walked over to him and kind of hovered.

"Um. Eh-hem. Hey, Daniel."

Without moving his eyes from the cell phone screen, he quietly replied, "Yeah?"

I sat down at the desk next to his. Poor guy — in a couple minutes I was going to crush his heart.

"How are things going?" I asked with what I hoped was compassion in my voice.

This made him look up. Blowing his bangs out of his eyes, he looked at me with what looked like panic. "What?" he asked.

"Nothing, I mean. What's up?" I asked, a little less smooth than before. I started getting nervous. Did I want to do this after all? What if I should give him a chance? Or what if it wasn't him at all?

Daniel put his phone down and kind of twitched. "Uh, nothing. What's up with you, Holly?"

He said my name! Totally thoughtful admirer behavior. Okay, here goes.

"Oh, nothing. I'm kind of annoyed actually. I think I have like, a stalker or something." I said this with nonchalance, carefully watching his reaction.

He furrowed his brow slightly, and then asked with concern, "Really? Is it serious?"

Hm. Not exactly the reaction I was hoping for. "Well, I mean, I'm not sure. He keeps leaving me creepy valentines and stuff. Like, poems."

This was it. I waited to see something register. Instead he put his hand on my arm and asked, "Are they harassing or threatening in nature?"

What the! This was not going as planned. "No, they're not threatening or anything. I mean, don't you think it's creepy? Would you ever leave someone a poem without signing your name?"

This was it. My eyes bore into his. And, aha! He was turning bright red as he took his hand back. "Um, well. I mean . . ."

I tried to smile compassionately again. "Daniel. It's okay, I won't force you to say it. But yeah, I know all about it."

His eyes widened. "You do?"

"Yes. I mean . . . duh. I just, I don't know how to tell you this but —"

"Does this mean Isabel knows, too?"

I paused. Excuse me?

"Isabel? What are you talking about?"

He clunked his forehead onto the desk dramatically. "Isabel! I know you guys work on the paper together. Does she know I've been sending her those anonymous e-mails?"

"WHAT are you talking about?!"

"What are *you* talking about?! Aren't you here to confront me about my crush on Isabel?"

My mouth dropped. Oh. Crap.

"Oh . . . yeah, of course. Uh . . ." I trailed off, my face turning red this time.

He looked at me pleadingly. "Please, *please* don't say anything. I was going to tell her at the Valentine's Day dance. I know she's a junior, so I don't have a chance. But maybe?"

I looked at his hopeful face and felt a lump in my throat. "No, of course not. Don't worry about it, man. Your secret's safe with me."

Then I ran back to my seat, on the verge of tears for some reason. I felt humiliated and . . . disappointed?

The rest of class went by in a mortifying blur, and when the bell rang I booked it out of there with lightning speed. I got to my locker and stood there with my head bent into it, digesting what just happened, when I heard the loud, excited voices of two girls next to me.

"Oh my God!" one of them squealed. "Guess who just asked me to the Valentine's Day dance?!"

"Who-ooh?" the other girl asked with rabid anticipation.

"Matthew Reynolds!"

Screeching ensued from both parties.

I froze, then pulled my face out of my locker nonchalantly and peeked to see who these girls were. Expecting to see some drop-dead gorgeous Amazonian freak from the volleyball team or something, my jaw almost dropped when I saw that it was this girl I really liked — Serena Mishimoto. She was a super talented artist and the teacher's assistant for David's art class. She always looked so cool with her choppy, blue-streaked hair and skintight black jeans.

I did not know this was Matthew's type. Although she looked like a model herself, Serena wasn't exactly a girl who fit into his group of douchebaggery friends. And who knew that she would be the type to squeal when a boy asked her out?

Then I realized that Serena and her friend were laughing. And not in a nice way.

"God, so what did you tell him?"

Serena scrunched up her nose. "I mean, what could I say? I was all, 'Ummm, I have plans that night.'" They both started cracking up and walked away.

Well, what do you know? Matthew Reynolds doesn't get everything he wants. Why did I feel so bad for him? Valentine's Day was proving to undermine the best of us.

After school the next day, Valentine's Day, David and I were sitting on the front steps of the school. He tossed a box of Sweethearts to me. I caught them with an "ewww" before I ripped into the box and read a lavender one that said "You wish." I snickered and tossed one to him that said "No."

While silently munching on the chalky candy, I thought about the three valentines sitting in my locker. The last one was delivered this morning:

Dear Holly,
   Happy Valentine's Day...
   ... Maybe Someday...
Love,
   Your Secret Admirer

Would I ever find out who it was? I snuck a glance at David, who was stretched out with his feet propped up on his skateboard — apparently without a care in the world.

Liz and Carrie walked up to us, each carrying a red rose. David and I recoiled at the sight of them.

"The hell are you guys carrying?" I asked, scooting away from them.

Liz pointed the offensive rose toward my face. "These are our Valentine's gifts to our Valentines — you two!"

David got up to run away from Carrie's rose and she chased after him, smacking his butt with it every so often.

I took the rose from Liz. "Well, although I am morally opposed to this sorta thing, thanks."

She sat down next to me. "So, any more clues?" she asked in a low voice.

I watched Carrie and David take turns batting each other with their rose — petals flying everywhere. "Nope. And in all honesty, I don't even want to know anymore. Whoever it is doesn't seem to be ready to reveal himself anyway." I looked at Liz in her cute Valentine's Day outfit: hot-pink shorts paired with a gray-and-white polka-dot cotton shirt. "What about you? Did you figure out if you're going to the dance tonight?"

Liz smiled slyly. "I decided to throw someone a bone."

"Who?"

"David's friend Steve."

"Pardon?"

Liz laughed. "I know, I know. But I actually thought about what you guys said. I can't be this picky. Plus, he's sweet. And . . . I want to wear a new dress, damn it!"

I smiled. "Well, I think that's nice. But, you know, just don't wear heels. Ha!" She hit me on the arm.

Carrie and David ran back up to us, both out of breath with red rose petals stuck in their hair. I started laughing. "Who needs Valentines with you weirdos around?"

BHS VALENTINE'S DAY SURVEY

WHAT'S THE MOST ROMANTIC THING THAT ANYONE'S EVER DONE FOR YOU?

My boyfriend, Chad (hey, boo!), brought a dozen long-stemmed roses and apple cider in champagne glasses to my cheerleading meet to wish me luck. It was soooo romantic. Then we totally made out.

— CHARLOTTA M., SENIOR

This really hot waitress gave me a free root beer one time. It was hot.

— ROBBIE B., SOPHOMORE

After the curtains fell on my final night of playing Juliet in *Romeo and Juliet*, Mercutio grabbed me and kissed me. Right in front of my boyfriend, the Apothecary.

— MILLIE L., FRESHMAN

I had a secret admirer send me e-mails, then show up at the dance with daisies — my favorite. We're going out now.

— ANONYMOUS, JUNIOR

APRIL

I've never had a talent.

You know how some kids at the age of four can win competitions doing triple back-flips and splits on a beam four inches wide? Or how about three blond-haired brothers all under the age of twelve who can play instruments freakishly well and therefore gather legions of prepubescent female fans? (I mean, how in the world did the Hanson brothers re-create Beatlemania in the '90s? Seriously.)

Well, clearly, I am not one of these mutants.

I've been thinking a lot about talent lately because of our upcoming spring Battle of the Bands competition here at Bay High. We've got some choice contenders this year — quite an eclectic mix. I always thought Battle of the Bands meant a competition between, you know, groups of kids who play instruments and stuff. But no, apparently the word "band" also encompasses the following:

- Five girls wearing fishnet stockings requiring POLES onstage to do a rendition of a song by some girl group with the unfortunate name of The Pussycat Dolls. Need I say more?

- A duo sitting on stools playing spoons. Spoons.
- Four freshmen who cumulatively weigh four hundred pounds doing a Dr. Dre medley.

In light of this competition, I've been thinking about where talent comes from. Are people actually born with these innate abilities or have they been beaten down enough by their parents and instructors so that they have no choice but to be good?

If you and I were forced to do flips off a vault every day of our lives, wouldn't we all be good at it?

Don't get me wrong. I understand that there's a huge difference between people who are really good at worthless things like baseball and people like Wolfgang Amadeus Mozart.

As someone who's never devoted more than one week to any activity in her life (minus being a reading nerd), I'm pretty appreciative of anyone who has abilities. So I'm excited to see what unfolds at the Battle of the Bands this year. Yes, I'm even excited for the spoons people.

See you all there. Oh, yes, and not to be biased or anything but . . . GO RAW MEAT DEMONS!

RMD-4-LIFE,

Holly

NINETEEN

BALLERINAS EVERYWHERE SO DISGUSTED THAT THEY'RE BARFING. AGAIN.

How I get myself into these predicaments, I don't know.

"You! New girl! You need to extend your legs! Don't bend your knees!"

Yes, that loud Russian-accented voice was talking to me. Me, the new girl.

I spun around to glare at Liz. She made an apologetic face and continued her tendus. I was seriously going to throttle her after class.

Ballet is on my Top Ten Nightmares List. Other items include wearing a thong, skydiving, touching a snake, and eating rabbit.

"Did I say thanks for coming already?" Liz whispered loudly to me.

"Yes. But that means nothing. I can't believe you actually convinced me to do this!" I hissed.

The class was terrifying. The teacher, Ms. Petrov, was this sinewy older woman who could touch the back of her head with the tips of her toes. There were fifteen other girls in the class who all wore leotards and tights and were stretching all seriously when Liz and I came in.

Liz was a walking American Apparel ad in her hot-pink leggings and ripped tank top. I was wearing yoga pants and an old PE T-shirt. We felt awesome.

But at least Liz knew what she was doing, somewhat. I felt like I was thrown into a laboratory full of scientists trying to find a cure for cancer and they were all looking at me like, "What? You don't know how to do science like us?"

"You . . . owe . . . me . . . your life!" I whispered to Liz between gasps for air. My arms were flailing at the bar and I was trying to mimic everyone's leg movements. This was one of the most difficult things I had ever tried to do in my life. Who the hell invented ballet? This was just torture disguised as art.

After suffering for forty minutes at the bar, we transitioned into floor exercises. What I like to call Humiliations: Part Two. This involved everyone doing spins across the room. One by one. I watched with sweaty palms as all the girls extended their arms and flittered in neat little spins across the room in a perfectly straight line.

I was next, before Liz, who nudged my terrified, stiff body with an "It's not that hard!"

Those four words echoed mockingly through my head as I spun into the walls, into the teacher, and into the bar. A couple girls giggled but I was so dizzy I couldn't tell who they were. I wanted to throw up and I had to lean against the wall to steady myself. It took all my willpower to not walk out of there. My only consolation was that I knew I would never have to step foot in this hellhole again.

"And now, ladies, we will work on some choreography for the last portion of class. Please stretch while I go over the one-minute routine you will all be learning for this month."

Routine?

Um.

I saw my life flash before my eyes. I was supposed to DANCE now? I knew it was dumb, but for some reason I assumed that ballet classes were all about standing in front of a mirror doing pliés. And that was hard enough.

I eyed the door leading out of the studio and contemplated making an escape. It wasn't that far from where I was. Maybe if I slipped out while everyone was stretching, no one would notice. . . .

Then I felt a hard jab in my shoulder. Liz shook her head and mouthed, "No way."

"There is no way that I'm going to actually *dance*," I whispered furiously as we sat on the floor pretending to stretch.

Liz looked aghast. "What?! What did you think ballet was?"

Before I could answer, Ms. Petrov clapped her hands. "Okay, ladies, let's get up and come to attention please!"

My chance to escape had passed. Panic rose in every inch of my body. I looked at Liz pleadingly. She tried to smile with forced encouragement. "Holly, it'll be fine. It's only like twenty minutes of your life." Nothing she could say would placate me.

"Let's go over the opening steps. The dance starts on the fourth count — one, two, three, and four." On the fourth count, Ms. Petrov swept her arms to the right and her feet moved with her. "So a balancé to the right, then one count, then on the second, we go into our glissade." She danced these two small movements — basically a sweep to the right, and then a little side jump to the left — and I was completely entranced.

Openmouthed, I watched her go through the entire routine — sweeping turns, hops, skips, and stretches. Each move was so graceful, so natural, so lovely. This wasn't anything like watching our dance team as they shook their butts and gyrated to outdated hip-hop music.

I was so entranced that I didn't even mind having to dance myself. It was definitely one hot, ugly mess — with me forgetting every step the second it was over. I couldn't keep up at all. How everyone else remembered the steps within seconds I don't know! Even Liz seemed to go into Weird Robot Dancer mode.

"New girl, don't forget to keep your arms in second!" Ms. Petrov called out to me.

Okay, how useless was that to say? Keep my arms in second? I could barely pay attention to what my feet were doing, let alone what the F my arms were supposed to do!

But it was sort of nice to see that she actually paid attention to me. I'm sure it was because I looked like a duck flailing its wings among a sea of beautiful swans.

Also, you know what? There was something awesome about dancing to classical music being played on a piano by an old man in the corner of the ballet studio. While I myself sucked royally, every once in a while I caught a glimpse of the girls around me dancing in perfect unison, and it was all very pretty.

And then before you knew it, Ms. Petrov swept her arms up and presented a little bow to our class. "Thank you, mademoiselles. Lovely class. I'll see you all next week!"

Everyone bowed to her in return (I just stood there looking confused) and then skipped off to grab their belongings.

"See, you survived!" Liz exclaimed after chugging water from her Sigg bottle.

"Um, barely," I replied.

"Well, either way, thanks for coming with me. Not sure yet if I'm going to stick with it."

"You should. I could tell it was all coming back to you."

"Yeah, right! Well, you honestly weren't that bad either."

I let out a snort of laughter. "I think it got better once the actual dancing started. That was kind of fun."

Liz raised her eyebrows. "Oh, really? You think there's a chance you'll come back next week?"

Before I could answer, we got caught in a traffic jam of girls trying to leave the studio. From one group of bun-heads walking in front of us, I heard a girl say, "I think people who haven't danced before really shouldn't be in this class. I mean, I know it's beginner and all, but it's like, embarrassing. That one girl was so hilariously bad." The girls next to her laughed.

It was like being transported back to elementary school. I felt that insta-gut-punch and had to blink a few times.

I looked at Liz instinctively. Her mouth opened to say something, anger flashing across her face, but I just shook my head adamantly. She ignored me and shoved her way between the girls, causing a few of them to trip.

"OOPS, that was embarrassing," Liz said with sarcasm oozing.

My hands flew up to my mouth to muffle my laughter and I skipped off after her.

TWENTY

TROUBLE BREWING BETWEEN
RAW MEAT DEMONS?

The noise was making my brain hurt.

No, it wasn't the banging drums by Oliver, who sat behind his drum set like Animal from *The Muppet Show*: flailing skinny arms, open mouth, and bouncing red curls as he smashed his drumsticks in unadulterated joy.

Nor was it the off-tune strumming from Karen's bass guitar. She played from behind a curtain of black hair, and her movements were so subtle that her lanky frame almost blended in with the background.

No, the noise that was making my brain hurt on a warm Sunday afternoon, just hours after my humiliating morning of ballet, was that of my two best friends, Carrie and David, fighting. Loudly.

They were set up in David's parents' garage, squeezed among tools, boxes of junk, and a disgusting sofa that I swear has been there since the '80s.

In the center of it all was Carrie. "YOU'RE GOING TOO FAST!" Carrie yelled with mike in hand.

"You're just too slow," David snapped. "Because you assume the song revolves around your voice." He was wearing his "band practice uniform": Ray Bans, jeans, a Clash T-shirt, and bare feet.

Carrie blew a strand of hair out of her face and said haughtily, "Well, yeah. I'm the SINGER."

"You're the singer in a BAND. Not a MUSICAL!" David hollered before slamming his guitar into its case.

Things weren't going so well with the Raw Meat Demons. It was only an hour in to practice and, honestly? It was pretty bad. They were bad even when they weren't fighting.

The thing is, RMD is usually really good. Their songs are fun and catchy and everyone likes to sing along to them. If anything, they always have a good time. But things were tense because the Battle of the Bands competition was coming up and this was their opportunity to be epic.

"Good luck beating Midnight Dawn playing your guitar like some mopey donkey on Prozac," Carrie spat as she brattily knocked the mike stand onto the floor with her camouflage-print Vans.

Oh yeah. And they wanted to beat Midnight Dawn — the current kings of high school band-dom at BHS. Actually, I wanted to see RMD beat Midnight Dawn, too. Midnight Dawn was made up of these total snobs whose parents bought them the best equipment money could buy — and the best vocal and music teachers, too. There were also rumors that they were getting signed to a record label. (I'm sure it had nothing to do with the fact that the lead singer's dad owned several record labels up in LA.)

So yeah, they were the band to beat. If Disney made a movie of this Battle of the Bands, Midnight Dawn would be that black-uniformed hockey team everyone hated.

"A mopey donkey? What the hell is that?" David was angry, but I could tell he was trying not to laugh.

Karen butted in timidly. "Also, Carrie? You can't start singing that early because we have that monologue from *Doctor Zhivago* in the beginning." She immediately disappeared back into her hair.

Oh, Lord. They're trying to be all literary and cool now. The same kind of crap that Midnight Dawn always pulls. *Doctor Zhivago*? Who the heck?

"KAREN LORENA CLEMENTS AND DAVID FU-HAN CHEN. This intro makes our song like, almost twelve minutes long now!" Carrie exclaimed.

"Twelve minutes?!" I screeched, almost falling off my stool.

"Yes, twelve minutes. It's going to be EPIC, remember?" David said testily.

"Uh, yeah, I heard you the first twenty times," I responded, matching his tone.

Carrie started packing up her things. "I'm over this. We're never going to get this right." Oliver and Karen were putting their stuff away, too.

"So . . . is that it? Your practice is over because you guys fight too much?" I demanded.

I was almost physically injured by the power of their combined laser-beam glares.

"I think this band is over. We suck," muttered David.

Oliver shook his head and said good-naturedly, "Man, that's not cool." Then he glanced at his watch. "Damn. All right, I'm out. See you dudes at school." Karen left right after him. Which left me and the two divas.

"Okay, you guys need a break. Burritos?" I suggested hopefully.

A few minutes later we were on our bikes headed out to the Burrito Shack. I hoped the bike ride would cool off Carrie and David. It seemed to work. When we hopped off our bikes we were pretty sweaty and out of breath.

"So are you guys going to be civil now?"

Carrie pursed her lips but reluctantly nodded her head. "Fine. Whatever."

"What she said," David grunted.

As we ate, I decided to speak up. "So, why can't you guys just perform one of your old songs? People love those songs. I mean, the last house party you played ended at 3:00 A.M. because people couldn't stop dancing and acting like idiots to your music." It was true. Not that I was really allowed to go to parties. But I had *heard* all about it.

"We want to transcend that whole party-band image, Holly," David replied in an irritating know-it-all voice.

"Yeah, we think we can make a song that is totally like, Arcade Fire times one hundred," Carrie said between mouthfuls of beans and cheese.

"Who cares about those Canadian hipsters?" I sputtered. Their jaws dropped — Arcade Fire was their favorite band. "You guys should be true to the spirit of RMD!"

David set his burrito down. "We're going to write an epic song if it kills us."

I honestly wasn't sure if they'd come out alive.

"Hey, guess who's here?"

I had just walked into my house and been greeted by my sister and the delicious aroma of Korean food.

"Justin Bieber himself?" I screeched.

Ann just looked at me. "No, not Justin Bieber. God, not even funny."

I rolled my eyes. "Get a sense of humor, Ann."

"YOU get a sense of humor. Anyway, Sara's here!" Before the words were even out of her mouth, she ran off toward the kitchen in excitement.

"Sara?! All the way from Chicago?" I ran off to follow her. Sara was our older cousin — The Doctor. Aka the family's pride and joy. I would hate her if she wasn't already my favorite cousin.

"Hey, Holls!" Sara greeted me from the kitchen sink, where my mother had already put her to work washing bean sprouts. She was petite, her shiny hair in a perfect top-knot bun. She was wearing one of my mom's hilarious aprons (hot pink with a giant panda bear face on it) over her crisp navy-and-white striped dress. I almost sighed with pleasure at how put together she was.

"Hi! I didn't know you were in town!" I exclaimed.

"Oh yeah, it was a last-minute trip because my best friend just had her first baby. Do you remember Melissa Dickinson? She used to babysit you and Ann sometimes."

"Melissa had a baby? Ew, you guys are OLD!" I remembered Melissa as a teenager who wore a lot of sky-blue nail polish and talked to her boyfriend on the phone way too much.

"Yeah, we are old. You just watch, though. One day you and Carrie are going to be talking about real estate and babies."

I shuddered. "Never!" Ann laughed gleefully.

My mom shook her head from the kitchen table, where she was chopping vegetables. "That's what you think, Holly! Actually, I hope to God you even have babies. Who knows with this one."

I made a face at Sara. "Come on, let's go talk in my room. Where my mother can't annoy us," I declared loudly.

"Yes, yes," my mom said. "I'm always annoying! Never you."

I fled to my room with Sara in tow. Collapsing on my bed, I groaned, "My mom killlllls me!"

"Yeah, I remember that phase. Believe it or not, years from now you're going to feel sorry for how you treated her," Sara teased.

"Are you joking? God, I hope I never get as old and brainwashed as you!"

Laughing, she walked gracefully over to my book-shelves. "Still reading like a maniac, I see?"

"Yup," I said proudly. "My one joy in life."

"Oh, please. What else have you been up to? I'm sure high school is full of mind-blowing excitement!"

"Right. If you only saw what I went through this morning."

"Why, what did you do?"

"My friend Liz dragged me to her ballet class, can you believe it?"

Sara smiled. "Actually, that's not so weird. You used to love watching my ballet recitals. Do you remember that?"

I was taken aback. "No, I don't remember at all!"

"You did. You used to come to the recitals with my parents because you loved them so much. I even got you ballerina books when you started reading."

I had a vague memory of that. "Weird, I totally forgot!"

"Anyway, I think it's awesome that you went to a ballet class. I wish I had stuck with it, actually. I loved dancing," Sara said wistfully.

"Oh yeah, now you're just a doctor," I said sarcastically.

She laughed. "Whatever. Let me just say this, lady. You're lucky because you can do whatever you want. You realize that your parents are pretty cool, right?"

I must not have heard her correctly. "Are you joking? *Cool? My parents?!*"

"Stop with the italics, J. D. Salinger. Yeah, your parents. I was going to be a doctor since the day I was born — I didn't have a choice. Your mom was bragging to me earlier, you know — about your newspaper column. She's very proud that you're a writer. My parents would have killed me if I pursued something more liberal artsy. Like, say, journalism."

I didn't even know how to respond to this. "Dude, I mean, you're a doctor because you're like, a genius. All of us younger cousins are completely screwed because of you. You realize this, right? And there's no way my mom was bragging. She never brags about me. Or Ann."

"It's because she's Korean. Bragging about your children is a big no-no. You know how they get around it though, right? All, 'Oh, I am so worried about Holly. She loves to write too much. You know she has a newspaper column, right? I cannot believe that everybody wants to read her writing, but I guess they do!'" Her impersonation of my mom was so spot-on that I had to crack up.

"Anyway, I'm excited to see where your writing leads you — it's a real talent! Can I get copies of your previous columns? And don't forget to mail me new ones!"

I looked at her skeptically. "Talent, really? Also, you want to read my column?" I thought of all the asinine things I'd written about this year. How I took so much pleasure in complaining about Pilgrims and school dances.

"Of course!" she replied brightly.

"It's not exactly the most mature example of journalism. . . . After all, I'm not the *gifted* one in the family, Sara."

Sara sat up and looked serious. "You're totally deluded if you think I'm naturally a doctor. I had to work like crazy. And do you want to know something? I don't love it. I've just become good at it. So imagine if I put all that effort into something that I actually cared about."

My jaw dropped. "You don't *care* about being a doctor and like, SAVING LIVES?"

She rolled her eyes. "Oh my God, I'm going to be a podiatrist. I'm not all *Grey's Anatomy*–style saving lives every day."

I shook my head. "But the point is, you're good at it. I don't know if I'm good at writing, I just like it. And clearly, I don't excel at any other activities except being an okay student and not failing out of school."

Sara laughed. "Okay, whatever you say, Holls. Don't you *enjoy* writing your column?"

"Well, yeah. It's basically a place where I can barf my opinions every month and feel all smug about it," I said with a shrug.

"Well, clearly there is a demand for that, uh, barf. And it's awesome that you enjoy doing something that may one day become your future."

My future? I couldn't, and didn't want to, think that far ahead. I just wanted to survive the year.

I jumped up and grabbed Sara's arm. "Okay, enough of this pep talk! Drive me to the new Ryan Gosling movie!"

Ann burst in at that moment and shouted, "Me too!"

"All right, you weirdos. Let's go!"

We happily followed the older, functional sister we never had.

TWENTY-ONE

. . . .

BHS FINALLY DISINFECTS CHAIRS FOR ANNUAL BATTLE OF THE BANDS

The auditorium was filled to the brim for Battle of the Bands. It was the one time during the school year when everyone seemed to contain at least a shred of school spirit, including myself. Liz and I were sitting near the front, and we were both pretty nervous.

"So, from what you saw, do you think they can pull off this 'epic' song?" Liz asked.

My stomach churned. "Well ... if they've practiced a little more since then ..." I trailed off lamely. Liz grimaced.

The curtains rose and the MC for the evening, Mikemaster Malcolm Ariza, said some unfunny spiel, and then introduced the first act: five girls dressed up as hookers from Hot Topic, lip-synching to The Pussycat Dolls. I glanced at the dad-like person sitting next to me and shifted uncomfortably in my seat. Damn these girls for putting us in this awkward position!

We had to sit through some pretty bad yet hilarious acts before the Raw Meat Demons came onstage. Two suburban boys rapped to the Beastie Boys' "Girls." (One of them ended the performance by ripping off his track pants and tossing them into the audience.) Another good one was the Schilling siblings, all seven of them with their wheat-blond hair and handmade clothes, lined up singing an acoustic version of some hit song by the Osmonds. The boredom was palpable.

And finally: "All right, everyone, here to perform their spanking new song, 'Apathetic Inferno in D Minor,' are THE RAW MEAT DEMONS!"

The audience roared in response, coming back to life after that last performance. I glanced around at everyone nervously because I knew they were in for a big surprise.

The lights dimmed and projected images of bare tree branches and birds flitting across a screen. Then came the obscure monologue from *Doctor Zhivago*. A few people in the audience murmured in confusion and I started to sweat.

One by one, each of the Raw Meat Demons came out onstage. They were all wearing black — Carrie in a mini-dress with tights and boots, David in a button-up shirt and jeans, Karen in a weird turtleneck/leggings combo, and Oliver in a T-shirt and slacks.

"What's with the black?" Liz whispered while getting her cell phone out of her blazer pocket, ready to record.

I shook my head. "More pretentious?"

Once they were all situated, Karen started with a few mournful, pretty notes on her bass, and Oliver soon followed with a mellow beat. So far, so good.

Then David and Carrie came in and that's when things started to go awry. First, Carrie started off with the lyrics:

A swivel of vowels
Come at the unsuspecting
Through it all
Bear, walk toward me

I held my breath as people started to snicker. Then things veered off into the bizarre — the song seemed to change and I cringed, knowing that one of their goals was to create a song like "A Day in the Life" or "Bohemian Rhapsody" — a song that changed completely halfway through. Somewhere John Lennon and Freddie Mercury must have been rolling in their graves.

Liz leaned over and whispered, "Good God!"

It got worse. I could tell that the band was starting to lose confidence, and little mistakes were being made here and there. Carrie flubbed a lyric and then Oliver dropped one of his drumsticks during a crazy drum solo.

The audience started to get ugly — some kids were yelling insults and booing. I whipped my head around furiously, ready to rip some throats out, when I heard Oliver yell out, "One two, a one two three!" as he slammed his drumsticks together over his head. He never looked more like Animal than at that moment.

He started playing "Killer Whale Love," the Raw Meat Demons' biggest hit to date. It's the song that everyone at BHS knew and loved. And it was stupid, silly, and short.

David and Carrie exchanged panicked looks, and then looked at me and Liz. We both raised our arms and whooped, "KILLER WHALE LOOOVE!"

And that's all it took. They went into the song full force, kicking aside some of the weird instruments and props they had lying around (like an accordion, for God's sake), and Carrie swung her hair, bouncing up and down while singing:

> She was a girl
> He was a boy
> But they were whales
> Woo ooh
> Whales!

Everyone started clapping and singing along. We were in a frenzy — kids who were moshing in the aisles had to be escorted out by sweating middle-aged teachers.

The band finished to a standing ovation and looked ecstatic. Liz and I stood up, cheering louder than everyone else. I spotted Carrie's mom in the crowd, throwing a bouquet of sunflowers at Carrie, and David's parents beaming and clapping enthusiastically. Although David's dad never quite approved of his music obsession, he looked pretty proud of him right then.

"I am SO glad they changed songs!" Liz exclaimed as we sat down.

"Me too. I mean, talk about epic. That was *totally* epic!"

But the Raw Meat Demons had one major competitor left: Midnight Dawn. And they were up.

The stage turned pitch black, and it was silent for almost a full minute. Then laser beams of neon pink and green shot across the stage, creating a hypnotic pattern. Fog filled the stage and the lights cut through it like lightsabers.

The audience *ooh*ed and *aah*ed. "Oh, big whoop," I said loudly. Liz snickered and the man next to me glared at us. Oops, must be a Midnight Dawn dad.

The lights on stage suddenly shone intensely, blinding everyone, and when we recovered our sight we could see seven guys wearing hipster preppy outfits — shrunken pastel jeans, Ray Bans, popped collars, socks with Vans, and some sported tortoise-shell glasses.

Liz made a face. "Yuck. Trying *so* hard. Someone must have told them that prep is in."

"I know, get outta here. The last show they were all leathered out. Who are they kidding? It's like a J.Crew catalog exploded onstage." The man next to me cleared his throat loudly. Liz and I looked at each other and tried to suppress our giggles.

Midnight Dawn continued to perform an echoey, ethereal number called "Looseleaf Memoir." I had to admit it was pretty, but it definitely lacked energy. The lead singer crooned in a falsetto with his eyes closed so lovingly that I expected him to start making out with himself onstage.

Also? The song lasted for eight minutes. Prettiness be damned, people started to get antsy.

The show wrapped up with one more act — a girl singing alone with a piano, which would have been nice except she forgot the lyrics to the Lady Gaga song she was attempting to cover, and the piece ended in tears. After she was rushed offstage, Liz and I nervously awaited the results of the competition.

"I think they might win," Liz said with excitement.

"Shh! Don't jinx it!" My superstitious Korean side always came out in moments like this. I knocked on the tiny portion of wood on my seat's armrest for good measure.

Mikemaster Ariza lined three trophies up on a table and announced the third-place winner — the five Pussycat Dolls. Yep. All the guys in the audience cheered raucously, and Liz and I shot disgusted looks at the ones sitting around us.

After clearing his throat, Mikemaster Ariza announced, "And the second-place winner for this year's Battle of the Bands is . . ." A silly drumroll came from somewhere backstage and the crowd tittered nervously.

"MIDNIGHT DAWN!"

There was an audible gasp from the audience, and Liz and I looked at each other, eyeballs bulging. Holy crap!

Midnight Dawn came back onstage, looking pretty stunned in their stupid outfits. The one in the bow tie looked particularly crestfallen.

Okay, so this didn't mean that the Raw Meat Demons

won. . . . But who else would, right? Liz and I clasped hands and jumped up and down like little girls.

"Now, the moment we've all been waiting for. Please give a round of applause for this year's Battle of the Bands champions . . ."

My heart stopped beating.

"THE RAW MEAT DEMONS!"

Carrie, David, Karen, and Oliver ran out onstage to get their trophy and started hugging each other and jumping up and down. I ran to take a picture of them, and they all lined up with the trophy held between them — sweaty and happy.

It was great.

I knew at that moment that it didn't matter if you weren't technically the best. I also knew that I would be going back to ballet class next week. And those catty dancer girls? Bitches better watch their buns.

LETTERS TO THE EDITOR

The Battle of the Bands was off the HOOK this year! We need more rap, though. I want to start a petition to have at least 45 percent of the acts be rap.

— JONATHAN G., JUNIOR

MIDNIGHT DAWN WAS ROBBED.

— ANONYMOUS, SOPHOMORE

Where can I pick up an album by the Raw Meat Demons? Also, David Chen and Oliver DeSoto are SO CUTE!

— VANESSA M., FRESHMAN

Where can I get the phone numbers of those pole-dancing chicks?

— STEPHEN N., SENIOR

JUNE

All of America needs to get over their stupid perceptions of what high school is like. Based on television shows and movies, you'd think American teens led THE MOST DRAMATIC LIVES EVER! Do people not remember what their own high school experiences were like?

Let me tell you about high school:

- Kids don't fall in real love. Nope. They don't. No one stares longingly into someone's eyes and says things like, "Stacey, you are the most amazing woman I have ever met, and I am so lucky to have you in my life." You know where you actually hear things like that? At weddings of thirty-five-year-olds. Not in the hallway at Bay High School.

- We do boring things. Not fun, exciting things. Boring, boring, boring. We hang out in malls trying to trip each other and laugh. We spend hours at Quiznos avoiding going home. We spend beautiful Saturday afternoons watching television shows about other people doing stuff. You know why? BECAUSE WE ARE KIDS. It's kind of hard for us to do fun things because we don't have any money or street savvy.

- Nothing is epic. No emotional indie ballad plays during some pivotal climax scene while we run in slow motion through hospital doors or across a football field. Kids don't stand stoically against an eerie backdrop of blue-and-red police lights as they watch their hot girlfriend OD on the street.

So, why is it that we high school kids insist on being disappointed by our own lives when they don't have enough drama? Why do we hold ourselves up to these ridiculous expectations? And why oh why does this expectation always seem to be at a fever pitch when the end of the school year rolls around? Guess what? The end of this school year? IT WILL BE LIKE THE REST. Summer happens. Then we come back. The End.

Predictably,

Holly

TWENTY-TWO

AS SCHOOL YEAR DRAWS TO CLOSE, WEATHER GETS HOT

Why is it that everyone expects something epic to happen at the end of the school year?"

David shrugged. "Because we're dumb, man. Hollywood creates these false realities and stupid teenagers aspire to them."

"'Man'? Are you going for a new stoner vibe now?" I shoved David as we walked up to my house.

"I can't help it if my speech is always ten steps ahead in coolness of yours, Hiz," he said with a condescending shake of his head. I opened my front door and was about to respond with something truly brilliant but was stopped in my tracks.

"Dad? What are you doing home?" He was standing in the middle of the living room with his driver in hand, practicing his golf swing.

"Oh, just came home early," he replied between swings. "Hi, David." David waved and said with Asian Child Politeness (ACP), "Hello, Mr. Kim."

"Why?" I demanded.

My dad ignored me and said, "David, studying hard this year?" His eyes didn't move from his grip.

"Yup, as usual!" David said in the cheerful voice he reserved for my parents.

"Good, good," my dad replied. And continued practicing his swing.

I stared at him. Why wasn't he answering my question? Also, I knew that when my dad practiced his golf swing like this, it only meant bad things. The last time was when our pet gerbil went "missing" and my dad avoided telling us Crackers had been dead for days. There was something he wasn't telling me, I just knew it.

I waved David toward the backyard. (I wasn't allowed to have David in my room, believe it or not. They've known him forever but a boy is a boy is a boy to my parents.) After dropping our backpacks in the dining room, we stepped outside and sprawled out on a couple of lawn chairs.

"Well, that's weird," I muttered.

"What, your dad?"

"Yeah. He's never left work early or even taken a sick day in the twenty years he's worked for the air base." My dad was an engineer for the Miramar air base — you know, where *Top Gun* took place. I love that a Tom Cruise movie is San Diego's claim to fame. That and a killer whale named Shamu.

"Maybe everyone went home early today," David suggested with a shrug.

"Maybe. Anyway, I, for one, am not looking forward to the end of this year, believe it or not."

"Why?!" David comically whipped off his sunglasses and widened his eyes. I reached my left leg over to kick his chair.

"Because. I have to go to SAT school this summer."

David shuddered and made a face. "Seriously, that will ruin your entire summer vacation."

"I know! Since my first day of high school, my mom's life has revolved around me conquering the SAT. You would think my entire future existence hinged on this one stupid, completely biased test."

David yawned and stretched out like a cat in the sun. "Yer preachin' to the choir, my friend." I stared out into the yard and felt like I was staring into the abyss that was my boring future. A pair of fingers snapped two centimeters away from my face, shaking me out of my self-pitying reverie. "Yo, Hiz-house, did you hear me?" I swatted his hand away.

"NO. Geez."

"I was saying, maybe with this craptacious summer ahead of you, we should do something epic. You know, live up to the hype in the movies."

"Like what?" I asked with (completely justified) skepticism.

"Liiiiike . . . skipping up to LA to see Hot Chip play at the Hollywood Bowl!" He was literally jumping up and down in his chair. Hm. Hot Chip was my favorite band of the moment. But LA?

"Even if I wanted to, no way in hell would my parents let me go to LA to see a show."

David rolled his eyes. "So lie to them."

"UM, easier said than done! Do you not know Mrs. Kim? She who can detect a lie within a ten-mile radius?"

"Pfft. I think we should do it. And not just go up to see the show, but stay there for the night. The show's on a Saturday so we can drive up early, and hang until Sunday! We can stay at my cousin Lawrence's apartment near UCLA. I've been wanting to plan something like this forever!"

Needless to say, the prospect of hanging out with chemical-engineering-major cousin Lawrence did NOT excite me. "Okay, D, what?! Why do we have to stay there? Hello, going up to LA with you guys is already pushing the Mrs.-Kim-death-wish-o-meter! A weekend trip? I might as well —"

"Yeah, yeah, yeah," David rudely interrupted. "You make excuses for everything. How long is your mom going to rule your life?"

"FOREVER! Do you not know me and my Korean girl curse? The curse is forever."

"Break that curse."

I almost started laughing until I saw that David was dead serious. "Holly, let's just have fun already. We can all hang out there for the weekend, away from this armpit of a town."

Geez. It's not like we lived in the middle of Kansas. And um, LA is like two hours away. You'd think we were traveling to Paris for a spontaneous getaway, the way David was getting excited. He was already pulling out his phone and texting someone. "You're so boring. I'm telling Carrie to come over, she will totally be down for this!"

"Boring" stung. It wasn't the first time I'd been called that. Sometimes it was hard being best friends with an Extreme Sportsman (David), a Hippie Outdoorswoman (Carrie), and a Professional Everything (Liz). I was the token Stick in the Mud. "I'm not boring! I mean, how am I supposed to pull this off? This isn't like, some rebellious episode of iCarly. I'll get caught quicker than you can say 'Omo.'"

"I'll figure it out. Leave it to me, Hizzle."

I snorted. "Yeah, okay."

David just shook his head. "Oh ye of little faith. Who do you think I am?"

"Count me out," I said stubbornly, crossing my arms.

"So is David staying for dinner?"

I was reaching over my mom's shoulder to grab a cucumber slice she'd just chopped. "No, I don't think so."

"Aren't you getting a little old to be playing with David all the time?"

I almost choked.

"Play?! What are you talking about? David's been my friend for four years. Do you have a problem with him all of a sudden?" My voice was lowered because David was in the dining room helping Ann with some math homework. My mom wouldn't make eye contact with me, and kept chopping the vegetables for the salad she was preparing.

"I don't have a problem. But you are getting older now, and David's a boy. What will other people think when you are with a boy all the time? Just alone, you two?" What was my mom saying?

"What is wrong with you? Why are you being so Korean and stupid?!"

Even before the words came out of my mouth I knew I had reached the point of no return.

My mother shoved the chopping block of vegetables into the sink with a huge clatter, and whipped around so that her face was inches away from mine. "You are a bad daughter!" she said in a dangerously low voice. I flinched. "I'm your mother and you need to treat me with respect! I'm not some trash on the street! So, say that again! SAY IT AGAIN!"

Tears pricked my eyes. "No!" I yelled back.

She stared at me with murderous rage for another few seconds before she turned on her heel and left the kitchen hollering, "Ungrateful brat!"

I was standing in the kitchen crying, pressing my shirt-sleeve into my eyes when David walked in awkwardly. "Hey, are you okay? What happened?"

I wiped my face quickly, embarrassed. "Nothing. I

mean, nothing new. I just don't *get* her sometimes! I think . . . I think I hate her."

"Aw, c'mon. You guys will make up," he said, shoving his hands into his pockets.

Ann walked in with wide eyes. "What HAPPENED? Mom is soooo mad!"

"None of your business!" I snapped. "Get out of my face!" Ann's eyes welled up with tears and she ran out of the kitchen, pushing past my dad.

"Holly! Why are you yelling at everyone? What's wrong with you?"

I wanted to die. I hated that David was witnessing this. He seemed to read my mind because he threw me a sympathetic look and backed out, saying, "I should probably go. I'll see you tomorrow. Bye, Mr. Kim."

My dad shook his head sadly. "Holly, you shouldn't fight with your mother so much."

"I didn't *do* anything! She's the one trying to control my life all the time!" I said between heaving sobs.

"Your mom is only trying to raise you right. You have to understand that it's all for your benefit."

"She needs to learn to mind her own business. I'm not some robot child who will let her control my life!"

"You'll have to learn to get along." My dad sighed. "Because now there's a chance I'll be laid off from my job, and we'll have to really support each other."

I felt like someone punched me in the stomach. "Laid off?" It was one of those grown-up phrases that terrified me. "Why?"

He shrugged. "I work for the government. They don't have enough money to keep the air base open."

"What?! B-but, we're America! We love wars!" I cried.

My dad shook his head. "Holly, stop being funny."

"So, does this mean that our family's going to go broke?" Whenever you heard of parents getting laid off, families were always moving to different homes. Or different cities, even.

"Nah. Your mom still has a good job. I'll find something." Although my dad was acting like everything was going to be fine, I felt a huge sense of dread . . . on top of the stress I already felt from my fight with Mom.

Worst day ever.

TWENTY-THREE

. . . .

TODAY, PLANETS ALIGN TO
SCREW EVERYTHING UP

Someone whistled loudly in the journalism room and all conversations came to a halt.

"Hey, we have announcements for next year's staff change!" Isabel yelled. We all gathered around in a hurry. "All right. After weeks of deliberation, both Mr. Williams and I have figured out next year's staff." Everyone murmured excitedly — these announcements were always highly anticipated at the end of the year.

"Okay, so first: I'll still be editor-in-chief next year." Everyone clapped halfheartedly. Because Isabel is a junior that was no huge surprise. "And because Amir will be graduating this year" — everyone made the obligatory *aw* noises — "our senior editor position is open, and the lucky journalist taking his spot will be . . . Holly!"

My mouth dropped open. A few people gasped, and heads whipped to look at me. Eep.

"We'll find a new copy editor next year to fill her spot. Um, how about a hand for Holly?"

Everyone clapped dutifully, but I saw a few skeptical looks being exchanged. Dude, I was with them. How the heck did I get chosen to be senior editor? That was just like, one step below editor-in-chief!

"Do I still get to write my column?" I asked feebly.

Isabel nodded. "Yeah, don't worry! Your column is what got you this position in the first place! We think you're definitely capable of more responsible waters." Oh boy, more responsibility.

Isabel made the rest of the announcements and I left the period not knowing how to feel. Could I *actually* get into this journalism thing? Would I even be able to handle it?

Liz came up to my locker as I was digging out my biology book. She looked dazed. "Oh my God. Holly, do you realize we're both taking four AP classes next year?"

"What?! But we don't figure out our schedules until orientation," I sputtered. Orientation was usually at the very end of summer, when we took our ID pictures and picked out our classes.

Twirling a long strand of hair around her finger, she said, "Think about it. You know that we'll take AP English and history for sure. And then I'm pretty sure you'll be in chem and Spanish, too."

I let that sink in. It was true. Despite being an utter tool in science, I'd been tutored diligently over the years by Liz and David and had managed to stay on the honor track all the way to AP, holding on for dear life by a thread. And although it would probably kill me, I still had to sign up for advanced placement so that I had a chance in hell of getting into a reputable college of some sort. Kids were freaks of nature these days. Good grades weren't good enough anymore. You had to be a freaking saint and do underwater gymnastics AND take every AP exam in the country. And that's just for trade schools.

Liz caught my facial expression. "Well, don't be all stressed about it! I'm just saying, wow. Junior year is finally upon us. The defining year."

"I think I'm going to be sick," I muttered. The bell rang and Liz and I bumped fists before heading off in different directions. As visions of AP exams and the SAT and general misery ran through my head, I bumped into Matthew.

"Holly, Holly, Holly." FLASH. Charm explosion. Man, how did he do it? So irritating.

"Um ... Matthew, Matthew ..." I trailed off half-heartedly.

"Where you headed?"

"The Tall Building." Yep, we get real creative over here at BHS.

"Hey, me too. Let's go!" And with that little command, I was at Matthew's heels trying to keep up with his gigantic jock-boy strides. He glanced over at me, and then did this thing that made my treacherous, stupid, weak heart flip:

So casually, so naturally, he reached out and gently lifted the giant biology book I was clumsily carrying in the crook of my arm.

"Damn, girl, this is heavy." Ah, music to my ears. My face flushed, and I shook my hair forward so he wouldn't see my embarrassing Victorian reaction.

"Yep. Bio. Lots of . . . sciencey knowledge."

He burst out laughing and I beamed. "Oh hey! Did you hear about Sean Woods' party in LA next week?"

Asking me that question was like asking me if I heard about Lindsay Lohan's next dentist appointment. Why in God's name would I know that? "Nope," I said nonchalantly.

"You should come. His dad's house up there is off the hook. Right on the beach in Malibu." Sean Woods was the lead singer of Midnight Dawn, the one with the record producer dad. I did not doubt his house was "off the hook."

I accidentally let out a snort of laughter, which Matthew seemed to take as a sign of interest. "Yeah, you and your crew should come up. I'll text you the deets. What's your number?"

I managed to squeak out my phone number, and when he had it saved in his phone he looked up and said, "Sweet. Catch you later, Holly K.!"

And with that, he looked at me with a quick and easy smile, handed me my book, and ducked into his classroom.

Flip, flip.

The waves crashed into my ankles and the water was reassuringly cold. I felt rebooted somehow. The ocean always did that for me — it was definitely a perk to living a bike ride away from the beach.

"Okay, so Lawrence is totally down." I craned my neck to look at David, beyond Liz and Carrie. We were all sitting in beach chairs lined up along the shore with our feet in the water. It was our favorite hangout once the weather got warm enough.

Carrie whooped. "Good ol' Larry!"

"Well, luckily, my second cousin, Meri, goes to USC for law school, so I've got my parents covered for the weekend," said Liz. Surprise, surprise. Liz's insane Persian family network has her covered in every city in the world.

"My parents are cool with it," Carrie said with a shrug.

I glared at her. "I hate you." She kicked some sand into my face.

"So? What's your story, Hizzle?" David looked at me expectantly. Carrie and Liz were also looking at me with irritatingly hopeful expressions.

"I don't have one. Because I'm not going." A collective groan rose up over the sound of the crashing waves. Holly Kim: Crusher of All Dreams. "WHAT? I can't, people."

Carrie frowned. "More like, you won't."

"Yeah, Holls. I mean, my parents are on the same psychotic level as yours, and I found a way," Liz pointed out.

"YOU have a million cousins that will cover for you! I have nothing legitimate happening in LA!" I was beginning to hate the sound of my own whiny voice. Which I normally took much pleasure in.

David stood up abruptly. "Why does your excuse have

to involve LA? Let's just keep it clean and easy. You can say you're staying at Carrie's, as usual."

"Yes! That is an awesome idea. You've slept over plenty of times and your mom doesn't call or anything," Carrie pointed out.

Now, here's where I have to fess up to something embarrassing: I am really, truly afraid of lying to my mom. Rewind to when I was six years old: I had scared the living crap out of my sister by pretending to be a witch.

"I. Am. A. WIIIIIIITCH!"

Screaming ensued. My mom ran in to see what happened, and I was standing there with my two-year-old sister red in the face, cowering in a corner.

"She fell on accident!" My arms were outstretched in a "What can you do?" position.

My mother proceeded to spank me with a wooden spatula. "Never. Lie. To. Me. Again! I WILL ALWAYS KNOW."

These words echoed in my head for the next nine years. And believe it or not, I haven't lied to my mother since. I mean, not a huge lie that would get my butt spanked again. Homecoming would have been the momentous occasion, but we all know how that ended.

Carrie looked at me suspiciously. "You're thinking about the witch incident, aren't you?"

"OH MY GOD, NOT THAT AGAIN!" Liz yelled.

David shook his head. "You are officially too big for your mother to do that to you now."

"That's what you think," I muttered.

I was deathly afraid of my mom. But. At the same time I also hated being left out of things. And my family right now was a huge mess. I could use a break from them for a weekend.

And I have to confess: I couldn't help but hear Matthew's invitation in the back of my mind. Not that I would go. But . . . the possibility was admittedly, and annoyingly, exciting. I let out a giant sigh. "Fine."

David whooped and whipped off his shirt, running into the waves. The rest of us were right behind him. Well, minus the no-shirt part.

TWENTY-FOUR

. . . .

LA TRAFFIC NOT SO BAD TODAY —
JUST KIDDING

My phone vibrated and I looked down to see a new text from Liz:

> Yo Holly we're outside. Ready or not! Bahahaha.

Meh.

I tried to drum up what tiny ember of enthusiasm I had. What was pooping all over this potentially amazing Muppet Caper–like escapade? Two of the people downstairs.

I shuffled to the living room where my parents and Ann were sitting around watching Korean dramas. Well, Ann was on her laptop. Her Korean skills have declined so spectacularly that she can no longer watch Korean shows or movies without subtitles. I guess that's what happens when your older sister speaks to you in English from the first day of your life. And by "speaks" I mean orders her to fetch water and Mint Milano cookies.

"Okay, I'm leaving now. Liz is here to pick me up. Um, because we're both sleeping over at Carrie's. Remember, I told you guys? Okay, yeah, so she's here. Bye! See you guys Sunday!" I ran to the door before I accidentally told them the truth.

But my quick getaway was slowed down by both my parents getting up to walk me to the door. This is something that may strike some people as pretty formal since, as far as they knew, I was just going to a sleepover. But it's this weird formality that Korean people have, and I have to say it's kind of a pleasant gesture that makes you feel special as you're leaving.

"Make sure you eat something. Every time you come back from that girl's house you are hungry," my mom chided. It took an inordinate amount of self-control to not say something back, but I had to be on my best behavior so that they wouldn't find some last-minute excuse to make me stay home. Also? Carrie's mom does tend to make small portions of chard and tempeh for dinner.

"Well, bye!" And with a meek, completely uncharacteristic wave, I managed to slip out. And through the shrinking crack of the front door, I thought I saw the tiniest flicker of doubt cross my mom's face.

I sprinted down the driveway to Liz's shiny red Mini Cooper. (Her parents were still mad that she wanted this car over the BMW they had picked out for her. Please read that sentence one more time.)

"Let's get outta here before my mom changes her mind!" I said between pants as I climbed into the backseat. Liz stepped on the gas and we left my street with a squeal. "Liz!" I screeched, gripping the oh-crap handle like my grandma.

"What? You said get outta there!" Liz replied with a devilish grin. Sometimes I thought she was actually a trained European spy who knew how to do things like drive across canyon gorges and seduce and poison world leaders.

"All right, who's got the tickets?" David asked, popping up next to me from the backseat floor where he had been hiding from my parents' hawk eyes.

"Check!" Carrie said, holding them up in a fist that also held licorice. I grabbed one from her.

David started bouncing up and down in his seat. "Sweet! Hittin' the road, hittin' the road, hittin' the —"

"SHUT UP!" Our collective voices vibrated inside the car. Carrie threw some licorice at him for good measure.

We blasted Hot Chip on the stereo with the car's top down. The wind whipped through my hair and as all the stress left me, I couldn't stop smiling. Holy crap, this was a great idea.

"Hey, Holls! You ready for the X Games next week?" David yelled to be heard over the music and freeway noise.

I nodded, holding two thumbs up. "It's going to be awesome! But can we *not* spend two hours on the BMX competitions this year?"

"No way, dude. Morgan Long is supposed to be off the hook! We gotta watch all of it," he protested.

Carrie turned around. "I can't believe you guys spent all that money on buying tickets to that thing!"

David nodded his head solemnly. "Believe it. You guys are going to be jeeealous!" Liz and Carrie had come with us last year but almost died of boredom, so it was just David and me this year. David had to wake up at 3:00 A.M. a few months ago to be the first person to buy them online.

"Your *mom* will be jeeealous!" Carrie responded.

I cracked up. There's nothing like a mom joke. Gets me every time.

We drove through Carlsbad and Orange County, stopping at an In-N-Out for lunch and a pee break. An hour later I could tell we had arrived in Los Angeles by the gray-blue color of the sky. Ah, the glamour of smog. I started getting excited — until we hit monster traffic.

"How do people live like this?" Carrie asked with disgust.

Just then a car full of guys in Dodgers caps drove up next to us and started making lewd gestures. "GROSS!" I yelled, shaking my fist at them. They all laughed and one of them started rolling down his window.

"Oh my God, Liz, keep driving!" I squealed. She jerked the wheel and cut off a couple cars, then coasted in one of the far lanes. I breathed a sigh of relief as we lost the Dodgers fans.

"Wow, you're so brave," David deadpanned.

"Hey, this is LA. People get shot over road rage here!" I said defensively.

"Okay, Fox News," he said. Carrie laughed loudly from the front seat.

"I hate when you call me that!"

Liz looked at us in her rearview mirror. "Do I need to separate you two children?" I stuck my tongue out at her.

There was traffic all the way to the Hollywood Bowl — even the line to park was long. All four of us were getting super antsy.

"I have to pee!" Carrie complained as we idled behind a million cars.

"Me too," chimed in David.

"Why don't you just pee your pants and shut up about it," I muttered. Needless to say, we were all pretty grumpy by the time we got out of the car.

"Ugh, my shorts are all wrinkled!" Liz complained. Everyone was wearing their concert finest — Liz in little black shorts and a heather-gray shirt that was cropped just enough to show a glimpse of midriff. A black, floppy-brimmed hat sat on her wavy curls. Carrie was wearing — gasp — a dress. A short lacy cream one with long sleeves and ankle cowboy boots. David . . . well, David was in his usual skater shoes, jeans, and hoodie. But David was David.

Liz had threatened to kill me if I didn't look nice that night, too, so I was wearing mint-green cropped jeans with a shrunken black blazer and black sandals. I felt border-line cute. A small part of me had dressed for the *possibility* of going to that party that Matthew told me about, but I had yet to get a text from him so I tried to squash those thoughts.

Our sour moods turned when we entered the Bowl. We found our seats, which were pretty far back, but any spot at this venue was breathtaking. Hills and trees were nestled around us and the gray sky was turning into brilliant shades of pink as the sun sank behind the hills.

"This is going to be *awesome*," Carrie declared. We sat down as the opening band came onstage and I prepared myself for some real live fun.

"I usually hate when bands only play their new stuff, but this is freaking amazing!" Carrie shouted. I nodded stupidly in enthusiastic agreement, a huge grin plastered to my face.

"Is someone having . . . a good time?"

I elbowed David. "Can you just, please, not ruin everything?"

He grinned at me, and for a second, I felt completely unsettled. David is cute. We all knew this. But I didn't ever, ever, EEEEEEEEEEEVER think about it.

However, that night, there was something kind of amazing happening, and that quick, truly happy smile made me see him with totally curious eyes. The bright stage lights created a halo around his messy, skater-boy hair. His infuriatingly white teeth, which never required braces like the rest of us losers, beamed. Hm, and was he wearing cologne or something, or was I being completely nuts —

"Holly Kim-izzle?!"

A very loud, very boy voice interrupted my disturbing thoughts.

Everyone's heads swiveled and there, two rows behind us, was Matthew Reynolds. He smiled and effortlessly leapt over seats to magically end up standing beside me. But not without a slight shove into David. Oops.

Startled, I couldn't say anything for a few seconds.

"Whoa, small world, right?" he asked, still smiling.

I laughed. Loudly. "Um, yeah."

"Love this band. Didn't know you were into them, too!"

I heard my personal peanut gallery snickering behind Matthew. "Yeah, they're kind of . . . one of my favorites."

He nodded with a grin. "Awesome." He stepped back and looked at me. "Wow! You look great. You should wear green more often. Super cute." I felt my burning face betray me once again.

"Oh, uh, thanks! I don't want to wear green *too* often — don't know if the boys would be able to handle it," I managed to joke. He threw his head back and laughed, which made me start cracking up, and I forgot my self-consciousness for a minute.

Until I noticed that my three friends were now openly staring at us. Before I could introduce him to them, Matthew said, "Hey, so you're definitely in for Sean's party now, right? I mean, dude, you're here." With this, he held out his arms in a way that suggested he owned not just the Hollywood Bowl, but all of Los Angeles.

Carrie piped up. "Party?"

"Yeah, in Malibu after the show. See you guys there? Hizzle, I'll text you the address!" And with that, he was leaping back to his row where his *Gossip Girl* friends were staring at us, slack-jawed.

"Hizzle?" Carrie made a face and looked at David. "Only D gets to call you that."

TWENTY-FIVE

. . . .

LADY GAGA RUMORED TO BE AT MIDNIGHT DAWN RELEASE PARTY; BUT THEN LEFT BECAUSE SHE HAS A LIFE

We could hear the party miles before we saw it. Or so it seemed.

"Where are we?" Carrie sputtered, staring at the brightly lit mansion spread out before us. Music was blaring and cars were parked chaotically all over the never-ending driveway and stretch of perfectly manicured lawn.

Liz managed to maneuver her car onto some off-road patch of dirt. We crawled out awkwardly, Carrie falling flat on her face at one point.

"Please say that wasn't vomit," she groaned while spastically wiping herself off.

"Vomit would mos def be the best-case scenario here," David muttered.

"We don't have to stay if it sucks," I said, eyeing the mansion nervously.

"We don't have to step one foot in there for me to know that it sucks."

Liz shoved both of us ahead. "Come on, you party poopers. We're only young once. Are we going to spend the entire night bitching?"

"It's our specialty!" Carrie announced cheerfully.

We walked into the house. Oh, man.

It was packed from top to bottom, and it was about a hundred and fifty degrees hotter than the warm summer night. Music was blasting so loudly that I could barely hear David cursing. And, bodies . . . so many sweaty bodies. Ew.

After a few bewildered minutes, Liz led the way. "COME ON! LET'S GET SOMETHING TO DRINK!" she hollered.

Another thing about me? I don't drink. Pardon me for not wanting to pollute my liver for another few years. I knew I had a boring adult future ahead of me, filled with various gross beverages to help me get through the day, so why start now? (I mean, coffee. Really? Does anyone really LIKE coffee? I'm awaiting the special news bulletin that scientists have discovered it's actually disgusting.)

And honestly, none of us drank. The only kids who drank in our class were the jock-brains and sad substance-abuse kids who we made fun of. But there we were. Surrounded by the very same. And if there ever was a situation that required a little something, it was this. As we made our way through the crowd, I recognized a lot of people who had already graduated from BHS. They were all drunk and making out with each other and acting like they ruled the place.

Man, get a life. There's nothing more pathetic than Super Seniors not getting over their high school glory days.

Liz somehow discovered a bucket of beers out on the deck, which overlooked the Pacific Ocean. But wait, I'm sorry, my view was obscured by twenty girls in bikinis jammed into a Jacuzzi.

"Duuuude," Carrie said. "Look at that one girl! Oh my God, tell me she's wearing bottoms. TELL ME."

"Oh man, she's not," David muttered, quickly putting on his sunglasses and turning around.

Liz and I craned our heads to get a better look when I felt someone nudge me from behind.

"You made it!"

My face was inches away from tanned, chiseled dreaminess. Wait, did I just say dreaminess?

"Hey, Matthew," I said cheerfully, oddly buoyed by his presence.

"Helping yourself to some Bud, I see?" Matthew directed that question at Liz, who was digging elbow deep into the nastiness that was a giant tin bucket.

She grinned. "Only the best."

He reached over, lifting her arm out of the melting ice. "Here, let me get it. Way too cold."

She looked startled. And then, I felt a little something. Because I knew that startled feeling when Matthew Reynolds touches you casually, or does something minutely gallant. And I sure as hell did not enjoy seeing Liz feel it.

He held out four bottles triumphantly. "Fresh out of the bucket!" We each took one, David more reluctantly. Before Liz could take hers, Matthew held it up. "Oh, these aren't twist-off."

"Oh, do let me." Liz smiled mysteriously, taking the bottle from him. And then she did this thing that yet again convinced me she was a trained spy. She took the bottle, leaned it against the deck railing, and used her other hand to do a little chop. And just like that, the cap flew off.

Matthew let out a low whistle. "Niiice."

Liz shrugged and took a long sip. All while keeping eye contact with Matthew.

What. The. HELL.

Just then one of the bikini girls slipped and fell right into David. "Oh my GOD, I'm so embarrassed!" she slurred drunkenly.

"Too bad it wasn't the bottomless wonder," Carrie muttered. We tried to help her up, David turning a bright shade of red, her dripping-wet friends stumbling over to help her out. For a guy surrounded by a dozen half-naked girls, David looked thoroughly miserable.

By the time we untangled the entire mess, Matthew and Liz were gone.

"Um, where . . . ?" Carrie asked quizzically. We looked around, but the deck was busting at the seams and I could barely keep my eye on Carrie and David.

"Great!" David shouted, pitching his full beer bottle into a trash can. Carrie did the same. "That was beyond gross," she said.

I stared at mine. "Probably not organic either."

"So did Liz go off somewhere with Matthew?" Carrie asked incredulously.

A little black cloud hovered over my head. "Well, they were like, insta-chums."

Carrie looked at me sharply. "Does that bother you?"

I felt both her and David's eyes on me, and for the first time in my life, I wanted my two best friends to disappear.

"No," I said brattily. "I just don't get why Liz is so into him all of a sudden when she clearly hated him up until five seconds ago."

"Oh my God, get over it," David said. "I'm over it. I'm over this. I'm out." And with that, he shoved his way into the house and disappeared from view.

"What in the! What's wrong with him? Why is everyone f-ing leaving us?" Carrie exclaimed. I felt tears surfacing. This was the worst idea.

As a naked freshman named Buddy streaked right by us with girls screaming all around, Carrie grabbed my arm and led me away from the deck and onto the beach.

"Okay, we have to find our friends and get out of this place," Carrie said through gritted teeth. I just let her drag me around on the sand, limp and defeated. She glared at me. "And you. Snap out of it. I don't know what's going on with you and Matthew, but you can't just wallow in some lame pity party."

"Nothing. I mean, obviously nothing, right? I'm like, nothing to him. And Liz, she's . . . well, she's a trained spy," I groaned.

"What?" Carrie shouted.

Before I could explain my theory to Carrie, I saw a flash of red-and-blue lights. And then I heard sirens.

Carrie and I stopped in our tracks. Kids started screaming and scattering.

"Holy crap, is that what I think it is?" Carrie looked at me with huge green eyes.

I was so shocked I couldn't respond. My sulky bad mood immediately evaporated and was replaced by utter terror.

TWENTY-SIX

. . . .

COPS RAID MIDNIGHT DAWN PARTY, AS NO OTHER CRIMES EVER HAPPEN IN LOS ANGELES

Carrie clutched my hand and yelled, "Run!"

We booked it away from the cops but ran into a wall of screaming, panicking teenagers. Utter chaos.

"EVERYONE HALT!" a loud voice boomed over a bullhorn.

And what did Carrie and I, obedient-to-the-end idiots, do? We halted. My palm was sweaty in Carrie's hand. My other hand . . .

"OH MY GOD!" Carrie and I yelled simultaneously. We had both noticed that I was clutching my now-warm beer in my other hand. We looked at each other frantically for a second before one of the cops walked up to me.

He flashed a light directly on the drink in my hand.

I almost fainted. Oh crap, oh crap. THE ONE TIME!

"How old are you, young lady?" he asked.

Tears instantly filled my eyes. "Um, fifteen."

Carrie stammered, "Sh-she was just holding it, I swear. We were just leaving!"

The cop shushed her and grabbed the beer from me. "Both of you, come with me." No handcuffs necessary, both of us followed meekly.

We heard people yelling from inside the house and saw other kids being dragged out. Other kids who were way more drunk than I was. If you could even call me that. I was sniveling, clutching Carrie's hand. She was patting my back and whispering, "It's okay, Holly. I mean, they can't arrest everyone. We'll be fine. We're clearly the good kids."

As we approached the car, we heard David calling out our names. I turned to see him and some other guy sprinting toward us.

"You stop right there, kids!" the cop bellowed, and they slowed down to a trot. David called out, "Officer, they're my friends!"

"He is, he's with us," Carrie said. I was mute. I didn't know how to talk anymore.

The officer rolled his eyes. "Whatever." We waved him over.

"Are you guys okay?" David asked, out of breath.

"No," I finally said between sniffles.

"Um, Holly was holding that stupid beer. . . ." Carrie pointed to the bottle sitting conspicuously on the hood of the cop car. The cop was writing something down on a clipboard. What could he possibly be writing about? "Two fifteen-year-old goody two-shoes followed me to my car and now I have to pretend to be doing something."

David looked at me anxiously. "What's going to happen?"

"I'm going to jail."

"You are not going to jail, Holly, geez," Carrie responded. But she didn't sound very convinced herself.

I examined the dark-haired guy next to David. He had on black-framed glasses, a sweater pulled over a collared shirt, skinny black jeans, and was nervously tapping one of his Chucks. He looked a little familiar. "Who are *you*?" I asked, more rudely than I had intended.

He looked panicked for a second, and before he could answer, David said, "This is Alex Garcia. We had bio together last year. . . . I ran into him earlier when the cops came."

"Hi, Alex! I'm Carrie," she said, practically shoving me aside.

"H-hi," he stammered. He avoided looking at her, and at me, for that matter.

"I'm Holly," I muttered, watching the cop out of the corner of my eye.

"Yeah, I know," Alex said nervously. "I mean, not that I *know* you but I know your column and stuff. It's . . . it's great."

I looked away from the cop for a moment. "Really? Oh . . . cool. Yeah, um, maybe I'll write a column about this?" I tried to laugh. He laughed really hard in response. Carrie not-so-subtly elbowed me in the ribs. I ignored her.

The cop finally looked up from his furious scribbling. "All right, I can tell you guys don't usually do this type of thing. You seem like good kids, so I'm not going to report you."

A huge swell of relief washed over me. Carrie grinned and whooped. "Thanks so much, Officer. You don't even know."

"You can just keep the thank-yous to yourself, missy. I am, however, going to call your parents. You should not be out drinking at your age."

Oh. Please take me to jail instead. PLEASE!

After getting our phone numbers, the officer started making calls. I slid to the ground and went numb. I was dead. Beyond dead. My corpse had already been eaten by maggots and I was now their poop helping decompose the earth around my casket. David and Carrie sat down next to me, and that Alex guy just stood there awkwardly.

The cop called Carrie's parents first and handed the phone to her after breaking the news to them. From Carrie's side of the conversation, I could tell that her parents were concerned but not necessarily mad. Surprise, surprise.

David's parents did some yelling, and he held the phone away from his ear. Then he muttered his good-byes and said he would be home that night.

"And you, kid, what's your parents' phone number?" the cop asked Alex. Alex looked as scared as I felt. He stole a quick glance at us and mumbled something. The cop put his hand up to his ear and said obnoxiously, "I can't hear you, son!"

Alex spoke up. "I don't . . . have parents. You can call my grandmother but you'll have to speak Spanish."

The cop cleared his throat loudly. "Well, there's no need

for that, I guess. Let's just move on to the young lady here."
Meaning me.

The world went into slow motion. I saw the officer talking but couldn't hear anything. Oh my God, did I just go deaf? I looked desperately at Carrie, who was watching the phone call intently. The officer scowled and handed the phone over to me.

"It's your mom. Good luck, kid." He grimaced. I shook my head frantically and his eyes widened. "NO," I mouthed. I'd rather face the wrath of this cop than my mother.

Finally, Carrie grabbed the phone.

"Hi, Mrs. Kim, it's Carrie. Everything's okay so no need to worry."

I could hear muffled yelling from where I was sitting.

"Yes, we are so sorry. She's so sorry. No, I don't think it's a good idea to talk to her right now. But we're safe. Liz is going to drive us home. No, nobody is drunk. Holly wasn't drunk. She just . . . It was bad timing. Yes, I'm sorry. Yes, my parents know. Yes, we'll leave right now. Good-bye. Huh? Oh, okay. Yes, bye."

Carrie handed the phone back to the officer. "Can we go now?" she asked, barely disguising her impatience. He waved us off.

"I'm going to text Liz," David said, pulling out his phone.

"What did she say?" I asked Carrie fearfully.

She took a deep breath. "Um, just a bit of 'Are you crazy? You are liars and bad, bad kids. You should have been arrested to learn your lesson. Get home now. You are in huge trouble.' And so on."

"Trouble" didn't even begin to come close to what was awaiting me at home.

"Thanks, Carrie." I was never more grateful for my most loyal friend.

She gave me a hug. "You're welcome. Don't worry, everything will be all right."

I started to cry into her shoulder, not caring that Alex was watching.

David walked over to us. "Um, Liz says she'll meet us at the car."

I nodded miserably. "Sorry, guys. Sorry I dragged you into this."

"Oh, please, you didn't drag us into anything. We wanted to come. At least we had our end-of-year adventure, right?" Carrie said good-naturedly. She punched David when he didn't say anything.

"My parents weren't that pissed. They'll get over it. So . . . no worries." He shrugged.

That was super comforting. Not. I caught Alex staring at me, and when I met his gaze he blushed and turned to David. "Well, I'm glad everything's good with your friends. I'm, uh, going to head back now."

"Cool, dude. See ya," David said with a wave.

When he was out of earshot, Carrie interrogated David. "Well, who was *that*? Why have you been hiding such a cute friend from us?"

"Uh, maybe because you're crazy and I don't want you embarrassing me," David said while walking quickly toward the car. Then he glanced at me. "Besides, I think he's into Holly."

Both Carrie and I stopped in our tracks. "WHAT?" we asked in unison.

But he wouldn't elaborate. Carrie basically climbed up onto his shoulders trying to get him to talk. "What do you mean? Tell us! You can't just say that and walk away!"

I jogged to catch up with them. "Yeah, did he say something?" I momentarily forgot about the death sentence awaiting me at home.

David let out a frustrated noise. "I knew I shouldn't have said anything to you nutjobs! GOD. SO ANNOYING!" He wriggled out of Carrie's death grip.

He stood there for a second, and I couldn't understand why he looked so angry. Then he looked straight at me. "Do you remember anything about . . . a secret admirer?"

Carrie gasped. My jaw dropped and my heart started pounding. I'd forgotten all about the valentines — it had been months and I gave up trying to figure out who it was after that awful conversation with Daniel.

"What . . . is he . . . did he?" I asked, my heart pounding in my ears.

David looked injured. "So it's true?" I had never told David about the valentines, and now I felt bad for keeping him in the dark. Before I could explain, he continued, "Anyway, he cornered me when I left you guys on the deck and kind of . . . confessed. I guess it was him?"

Carrie screamed in delight at the same moment we

walked up to the car where Liz was waiting with Matthew Reynolds.

I looked at them, then at David and Carrie, then thought about my mom waiting up for me . . . and ran into the bushes and threw up.

"Oh my God, how much did she have to drink?" Liz asked with concern as she ran over to me and rubbed my back. I pushed her off. I didn't want Liz's mature nurturing right now. I just wanted everyone to leave me alone.

"I'm fine. I'm not drunk," I said, straightening up. There was no way I could even look in Matthew's direction. I just walked straight to the car and got inside. I closed my eyes and tried to doze off.

When I walked through my front door, I was exhausted and so unprepared for what awaited me. And what was it exactly that I walked into? I kid you not, it was my mom bonking me over the head with a plastic hanger. If I wasn't so shocked, I would have laughed.

"Mom!" I screeched, batting the hanger away.

"You." Bonk. "Are." Bonk. "A." Bonk. "LIAR!" Bonk.

"Stop!" I whined, running away from her.

"You drove up to LA?! You LIED to me?! AND THEN! The POLICE called me? Do you know what I was imagining happened to you?!" she screamed rapidly in Korean.

At this point, Ann came into the living room. "Mom, stop!" she pleaded. The only time my sister and I ever teamed up was when our mom was yelling at one of us.

Mom stared murderously at my sister. "You stay out of this. Or you're next!" That shut Ann up, but she stayed in the room.

"I can't trust you anymore! Look what's happening to you! You're not the same daughter!" Mom cried.

For the umpteenth time that week, I felt the tears rising. "I only lied because I knew you wouldn't let me go!"

"OF COURSE I wouldn't! WHO WOULD? Only a bad parent!"

"You mean like Carrie's parents?" I yelled.

"They're American. They don't count. What Americans do with their children is up to them. You are my child! You follow my rules!"

I saw red. "YOUR RULES ARE CRAZY!"

My mom threw the hanger down and said calmly, "You are grounded. For the entire summer. You will only leave the house for family events and SAT school."

"Fine! Whatever!"

Her shoulders slumped, and for a moment I thought I had gone too far. Before I could try and remedy the situation, she turned on her heel and stomped back to her room and slammed the door.

I sniffled, holding back my tears as best I could. My brain couldn't digest anything from tonight. Ann stood by me, awkwardly trying to console me. "Sorry, I tried to calm her down but she threatened to kill me." A little laugh escaped between my sobs.

"Where's Dad?" I finally asked.

"He went to hang out with our uncles. He got laid off," she said sadly.

"What? It actually happened?"

Ann nodded and looked like she was on the verge of tears. This was when my big-sister instincts kicked in. I tried to smile and sound reassuring. "It's okay, Ann, we knew it was going to happen. Mom and Dad have a plan. We'll just have to try and be more helpful."

Her eyes were still watery but she swallowed and appeared to feel better. "Okay."

Be more helpful. I felt a wave of guilt. While I was drinking beer at a stupid party in LA my parents had probably been stressed out over the layoff. Maybe my mom was right — I was turning into a bad daughter.

I walked down the hall toward my parents' room, standing outside the closed door apprehensively. I knocked once, lightly. "Mom?"

There was no answer. "Mom?" I called again, a little louder. Still no answer.

I cracked open the door to see the room dimly lit by a bedside lamp, my mom sitting on the edge of her bed on the phone.

She was speaking in Korean, in a voice I recognized as one reserved for her parents. "I know. . . . It's going to be fine. . . . No, the girls will be fine, too. . . . I *know*. . . . Okay. Yes . . . I know, we should have thought of these things ahead of time. . . . You're right." I heard defeat in her voice, and she looked so small sitting by herself on the king-size bed.

Maybe I wasn't the only one who let her parents down all the time. I let a few seconds pass after she hung up the phone. "Mom?" I said cautiously.

She held her head in her hands and her voice was muffled when she said, "Holly, I don't want to talk about this any more until your dad comes home. Go to bed."

I walked in and sat down next to her. "I'm sorry. Sorry I lied." I swallowed. It was really, really hard to say these words to my mom. I was always trying to prove *she* was wrong about everything.

My mom was silent for a few seconds before she said in a tired voice, "Okay."

I started crying. "No, I really am sorry. I shouldn't have done it. I'm *sorry*. I've just been so . . . frustrated and mad!"

Surprisingly, all the stress from the last few weeks seemed to lift off my shoulders with those words. It had been a long time since I cried to my mom about anything.

She stroked my hair. "I know it's hard. It's okay, Holly. It's okay." And while there was a world of things that could be said between us, those few words managed to keep us both afloat for that night.

"Oh my God, did you see how tacky Gretchen's earrings were? I mean, where does she think she is, *Riverside*?"

I stared at the TV. I was about to throw the remote control into the face of one of the cackling witches on *The Real Housewives of Orange County* when the doorbell rang. Thank God! Rescued from reality-TV hell.

No one else was home so I ran to the door. "Who is it?" I called.

"Your mom. Here to beat you up with a coatrack," David's muffled voice said from behind the door.

I swung it open to see Liz, Carrie, and David standing on the doorstep. I recoiled against the sun. "Ugh, I haven't seen daylight in two days."

"Well, we're here to bring the sunshine back into your life," Carrie said optimistically. She whipped out something from behind her back and presented it to me.

I looked at it and squealed, "Beatles Rock Band?!"

"Yup, landed in my mailbox today."

"But, I don't have Rock Band," I said, puzzled.

Liz and David looked at each other, then stepped apart, revealing the entire Rock Band instrument set — including drums.

My jaw dropped. "Dude."

"I brought my set over since you're spending your entire summer watching — is that *Real Housewives?*" David asked with disgust, peering over my shoulder.

I rolled my eyes. "Yes. Kill me now. There's nothing on TV."

"Oh man, then let's switch it to ESPN. The X Games are coming on soon!" David exclaimed.

"Fine by me!" I said, happy to finally have some company. We carried all the Rock Band gear into my living room, where I had been camping out for the first couple days of my wonderful summer vacation.

"So, you're allowed to have us over, right?" Liz asked, plopping down on the sofa.

"Yeah, I'm just not allowed to go anywhere. Ever," I said dully.

Carrie waved her hand dismissively. "Whatever. Your parents never really ground you. They always feel bad eventually and cave after a couple weeks."

"True. But this was the most pissed my mom's ever been! My summer is going to be hell. I can't believe I was dreading junior year. School seems like a freaking gift from the gods now."

Liz's phone beeped and she pulled it out to read a text. Her eyes flew up to look at me.

"Is that Matthew?" I asked.

Liz smiled uncomfortably. "Yeah."

During the last couple weeks of school, Liz and Matthew had started talking and hanging out. It was still a little awkward between Liz and me because of it, but I was dealing with it. If Liz was into him then who was I to say anything? I really had no right to be upset about anything — it's not like Matthew had ever liked me. And Liz had been really sensitive about it, asking me if it was okay. I felt stupid, giving her "permission" like some jilted older sister from a Jane Austen novel.

Now that summer had started, they were spending more and more time together. And I guess texting each other constantly, too. Oh well. I just hoped she didn't start hanging out with his lame friends.

Plus, I had other concerns on my mind. Like Alex. Who I hadn't heard a peep from, or even seen at school since the party. And David refused to bring him up again. Carrie, Liz, and I had spent hours speculating and reliving those valentines until I was seeing love letters whenever I closed my eyes. What kind of secret admirer admitted to their love and then just vanished? Was David making this up?

"I'm going to get us some ice cream," I said, walking into the kitchen.

As I was reaching for my favorite seafoam-green bowls, David walked in. "Hey, can I have some water?" he asked.

"Of course. Help yourself."

"Cool." He opened the fridge for the pitcher of water.

As he poured himself a glass, something David had said earlier hit me. "Wait! Did you say you wanted to watch the X Games on TV?" It just occurred to me what day it was.

David nodded. "Yep."

"You're not going anymore?!" Clearly, I had to give up my ticket because I was grounded, but David had never mentioned not going himself.

"Nope."

I stared at him. "What are you talking about? Did something happen to your ticket?"

"Nah. I just decided not to go after all," he said, shrugging.

This was like a crackhead saying no thanks to crack. Who was this person?

"WHAT? How come?!" If I didn't know any better, I would have thought that David was blushing. "Weeeeell?" I pressed.

He cleared his throat and tried to answer nonchalantly. "Because. I didn't want to go alone."

I stared at him again. "But you could have given my ticket to someone else."

He sighed. "Holly. Get over it. I'd just rather play Rock Band with you guys today."

"Huh?"

"I think . . . it's important." And with that, he walked out of the kitchen.

I blinked once. Then twice. What was happening to my life? I went back into the living room with the bowls and spoons.

"Ice cream?" I asked. They all scrambled over to me, shoving each other to get to it first.

Well, some things don't ever change, I guess.

SINCE YOU ASKED . . .

A w, the last Holly column of the school year. Wipe those tears away. (Tears of happiness for some of you.) I'll see you all soon enough.

Don't expect the typical cheesefest of reminiscing about what an awesome year it's been. This year has not been the awesomest. While I'm grateful for this column and the joy it brings all of you, there were definitely some misadventures along the way.

Being hated by 80 percent of the school? GOOD TIMES!

Being accused of rigging the stupid Homecoming Court? AN HONOR!

Spending the holidays in Las Vegas? HEARTWARMING!

Almost getting arrested at a gross party in LA? PRICELESS!

But the upside to surviving this year? The anticipation of being a junior! No more being a second-class citizen. Instead, I'll enter the upper echelon of lame high school society.

In order to get there, however, I'll have to be tortured by an entire summer of SAT school and spend way too much time with my family.

It's been an interesting year. This column has definitely taught me a thing or two:

- Never insult the student government or they will try and get you expelled. Actually, scratch the "never" part. Because guess what, guys? You have always been and will always continue to be a bunch of humorless babies. I look forward to new battles next year.
- Sometimes you're the only one who thinks you're funny.
- The Homecoming Court IS a dumb tradition.
- Sometimes people are more than who they seem to be at school. They might surprise you, for the better.
- Korean people are not alone in celebrating Christmas in the desert. People of all colors with bad taste do it, too.
- Teenage couples take offense when you belittle their feelings. Boo hoo.
- A drama-free life is totally underrated. It's only when you have drama that you appreciate being boring.

So here's hoping for a decent year of surviving AP classes, enjoying off-campus lunch, and acting stupid with friends.

Because, really, they're the only ones worth

it all in the end. Do you think you're going to remember a dumb high school party thirty years from now? No, you'll remember shooting lemonade out of your nose when your best friend accidentally farted on you.

Congrats to the class of 2013. Good luck in all your future endeavors, whether they be college, unexpected pregnancies, or managing the Fashion Valley Banana Republic.

Until September,

Holly

ACKNOWLEDGMENTS

Thank you to so many people who have supported this book from its inception many years ago: Amy Kim Kibuishi for her wholehearted recommendation to our agent and her buoying support ever since. Kazu Kibuishi for letting me work in his inspiring studio. Kean Soo for his manly crush-worthy handwriting. Ginee Seo for helping me so early in the process. The Explosion staff from the years 1997–1999 — dorkiest/coolest journalism kids ever. To some of my favorite people and earliest readers who have always encouraged me to write — the inspiration for the friendships in this book: Natalie Afshar, Katherine Ahn, Chris Ban, Maya Elson, Emma Goo, Katee and Lily Kazeminy, Jennifer Li, Erica Pak, and Jill Russell.

Thanks to my agent, Judy Hansen, for her faith in me and her relentless hard work on behalf of me and many of my friends. Crazy thanks to my editor, Cassandra Pelham, who is younger but so much wiser than me.

To all my grandparents, aunts, uncles, and cousins who were integral to my childhood but never really as annoying as Holly's family. To Kristi and Tony Appelhans, for reading and caring. To my sister, Christine, who suffered under my teenage years and somehow never killed me. To my parents, for enabling my lifelong reading obsession and always supporting my decisions even when they made me very poor.

And finally . . . to my husband, Chris Appelhans, who inspires me to be *better*. Who sat next to me as I wrote the first line of this novel and who yells at me to get off iChat when I'm supposed to be writing. Who is the most talented and best human I have ever met. Thank you.

ABOUT THE AUTHOR

Maurene Goo was born and raised in Los Angeles, California, where she navigated her childhood by practicing extreme bossy lord-dom over her many cousins. She studied communication at the University of California, San Diego, and received a master's degree in publishing and writing at Emerson College. She lives in Los Angeles with her husband and a very old cat. You can visit her online at www.maurenegoo.com.